PRESENCE OF MIND

Anthea Fraser

Chivers Press • G.K. Hall & Co.
Bath, England   Thorndike, Maine USA

This Large Print edition is published by Chivers Press, England, and by Thorndike Press, USA.

Published in 1997 in the U.K. by arrangement with Severn House Publishers Ltd.

Published in 1997 in the U.S. by arrangement with Chivers Press, Ltd.

U.K. Hardcover   ISBN 0–7451–3053–9 (Chivers Large Print)
U.K. Softcover   ISBN 0–7451–3054–7 (Camden Large Print)
U.S. Softcover   ISBN 0–7838–8254–8 (Nightingale Collection Edition)

The text of this Large Print edition is unabridged.
Other aspects of the book may vary from the original edition.

Set in 16 pt. New Times Roman.

Printed in Great Britain on acid-free paper.

British Library Cataloguing in Publication Data available

Library of Congress Cataloging-in-Publication Data

Fraser, Anthea.
   Presence of mind / Anthea Fraser.
     p. cm.
   ISBN 0–7838–8254–8 (lg. print : sc : alk. paper)
   1. Large type books.   I. Title.
[PR6056.R286P69   1997]
823'.914—dc21
                                              97–14757

PREFACE

It's a delight for me to see this book, which I wrote more than fifteen years ago, back on the shelves.

It was an interesting experience reading it again after so long, and I was struck by the change in social behaviour which has taken place. The seventies was a more polite era, when, unlike today's unthinking intimacy, strangers did not call you by your first name until invited to do so and young people invariably addressed those of their parents' generation as Mr or Mrs So-and-so. And of course there was the absence of so many things we now take for granted. Today, Moira would have a word processor rather than a typewriter.

At that time, before I had a regular setting for my novels, part of the fun of starting a new one was choosing its location. Suffolk was a county I didn't know but of which I'd heard a great deal, and choosing it as a background for this book gave me the excuse of visiting it for a few days. And I loved it—the huge, Gothic 'wool churches', the pastel-coloured houses, the ancient towns with their quaintly named streets.

The house in the story, Fairfield Lodge, was based on one I saw illustrated in a glossy

v

magazine, and it was a help to have the pages in front of me and be able to picture my characters going in and out of the rooms or walking across the lawn.

In fact, I have a large 'Faces and Places' file into which I slip newspaper photographs and pictures from the colour supplements which I feel might be of use in a future book; and when in due course I've finished with them, I stick them in a scrapbook labelled, for example, 'Lance in *Presence of Mind.*'

At that time, I was fascinated by the idea of split personalities—the medical phenomenon known as hysterical dissociation. A true story on the subject, 'The Three Faces of Eve' (Thigpen & Cleckley), had been made into a film. Another, 'Sybil' (Flora Rheta Schreiber), detailed the *seventeen* different personalities of one woman, each ignorant of the others. Was this, I wondered, the origin of the ancient fear of possession? I leave you to decide for yourself!

I do hope you will enjoy reading *Presence of Mind* as much as I enjoyed writing it.

Anthea Fraser
Summer 1994

PROLOGUE

There was a burning sensation behind his eyes and he gripped the steering wheel whitely in an attempt to still the trembling which threatened to disintegrate him. It just wasn't possible. Not now, after all that had happened. *Don't let her die!* He had no idea to whom he addressed this plea, but it was more command than supplication. Just don't let her die, that's all! And then, as an agonised, superstitious afterthought—*Please!*

His brain shuddered away from the mere possibility. Appendicitis wasn't serious anyway, he told himself defiantly. It was just like having a tooth out these days. But apparently there were complications— peritonitis, a persistent temperature, and increasing lassitude. There had been no mistaking the unspoken fear in Mrs Cameron's quiet voice over the telephone.

'It's a fine time for you to be ringing,' she'd said bitterly, and the rider 'when it's too late' leapt over the wire between them, piercing his eardrum with a vicious jab.

'I'll go at once—I must see her!' he had stammered, and she'd answered with weary hopelessness, 'They won't let you.'

But they would, if he had to force his way to her bedside.

1

A lorry swooshed past with a warning blare of its horn and he realised he was weaving erratically about the road. Gritting his teeth, he fought the wheel to straighten the car again. This was the stretch of road along which he had taught her to drive. Another throbbing memory: there was no escaping them.

It had all been such a ghastly mistake. Somehow he had to make her understand that. Not only the mix-up over the picture, but allowing her to leave the way she did. It was only after she'd gone that he realised how much he loved her, and by that time pride and a niggling sense of shame had prevented him from contacting her.

Impatiently he waited for the traffic lights to change. The first thing, of course, was to tell her about the prize. Then they'd have to decide the best way of explaining the mistake, that it wasn't his work at all. It would be embarrassing, but it would have to be done as soon as possible, before there was much publicity. The ridiculous thing was that he hadn't even seen the painting until that very morning. If he had, he'd have known straight away that it would have to win. It was the most wonderful painting he'd ever seen. He had never dreamt Ailsa could achieve something like that. The most ironical thing of all was that she'd done it for him, for his birthday, and made him promise not to look at it.

'It's far and away the best thing I've done,

Jamie,' she'd remarked once.

'Then why don't you enter it for the competition?' he'd demanded truculently, glaring at the empty canvas in front of him.

'You know quite well why! Firstly it's *your* picture, and secondly I submitted my entry weeks ago.'

His picture. That had been the root of the misunderstanding. They'd always called it that. 'How's my picture coming along?' He could see her now in the studio they shared, head tilted critically on one side, her red-gold hair blazing like some exotic chrysanthemum above the pale stem of her neck. Oh God, why did he ever let her go?

It had all been Anderson's fault. 'We're getting concerned, laddie. The competition closes next week. It's not like you to leave it to the last minute.'

'I tell you it's no good,' he'd answered furiously. 'Nothing will come. Don't you think I've tried? For months now I've been starting on one canvas after another. Nothing will come.'

The keen eyes had regarded him under bushy brows. 'Then how about some of your older work? Hell's teeth, man, it's almost a foregone conclusion that you'd win the thing! You can't just throw it away! Let me come and have a root round. We're bound to come up with something.'

'I've a lecture this evening, but you can look

if you like,' he'd said carelessly, tossing him the key to the studio. If only he'd realised, then, what he was throwing away.

The hospital loomed up, grey and forbidding, on his right and he swung across the road without a signal, not even hearing the screech of tyres as the bus immediately behind swung desperately to avoid him. Robert Burns Ward, Mrs Cameron had said. Even that seemed an act of spiteful fate. With a spasm of pain he closed his mind to the memory of her soft singing. The stomach-sinking smell of the hospital, compounded of disinfectant and a recently finished meal, filled his nostrils as his eyes raked the direction board. First floor. He didn't wait for the lift but went up the stairs two at a time.

'Miss Cameron?' he demanded of the first nurse he saw.

She turned her stiffly starched head. 'No visitors, I'm afraid. Only parents. I'll tell her you called.'

'But I have to see her!'

Something of his desperation communicated itself to the woman and she hesitated. 'Would your name be Jamie?'

The name leapt at him over the intervening months. It seemed an eternity since he had heard it, had held her close and felt her calm, loving confidence flowing into him. He said past the obstruction in his throat, 'That's what she calls me, yes.'

4

'Aye. Well, she's been speaking of you. Two minutes, then. Her bed's in the far corner, behind yon screen.'

He scarcely paused to thank her. Two minutes! As if he could say all that had to be said in two minutes! He strode between the rows of high iron beds, each with its chart at the foot, his eyes fixed on the screen at the far corner, yet when he reached it he had to brace himself to go round it and as he did so all the fears he had been so frantically suppressing rushed over him again in an icy deluge. The limp figure on the bed bore little resemblance to the Ailsa he had known. The almost transparent skin stretched tightly over the prominences of nose and cheekbones making an unfamiliar mask of her small, pointed face. Some obscene contraption was rigged up beside the bed and from it a tube led into her bandaged arm, pitifully thin and childlike on the coverlet. And her hair, her vibrant red-gold hair, spread across the heaped pillows in a dull, lacklustre mat.

'Jamie?' The voice was soft enough to have been in his own head, but it brought his attention swiftly back to her face, to the cavernous grey eyes which, now open, regarded him. With difficulty the white lips curved into a smile. 'I knew fine you'd come.'

'Ailsa!' He pulled a nearby chair close to the bed and reached for her free hand, fragile and birdlike inside his, trying desperately to

5

transmit some of his own pulsing lifeforce into her frail spent body. 'Listen, sweetheart, the competition results are out. Have you heard? It won, Ailsa! Your painting!'

A shadow crossed her face but she still smiled. '*Your* painting!' she corrected in a whisper.

He felt the blood suffuse his face. 'You do understand that I didn't realise what would happen? If I'd only seen it beforehand—'

'Hush, Jamie, I know.'

'But that's why you left, isn't it? You said it didn't matter, but it did.' She moved her head slightly in a negative motion, her eyes straining to his face as though she knew it was the last time she would see it. Helplessly he sat holding her hand and his mind slid back again. The phone had been ringing when they got back to the flat that night, and for a moment he hadn't known what Anderson was talking about.

'Laddie, it's fantastic! I should have known you were bluffing, letting us get steamed up when all the time you had this up your sleeve!'

'Just a minute,' he'd broken in. 'I don't understand. What's fantastic? There's nothing—'

'*Eternal Spring*, that's what! Come on, boy, the game's over! You must know how good it is.'

'*Eternal Spring?*' he'd repeated blankly. The name meant nothing to him, but at his side Ailsa's attention had been caught. He'd raised

6

his eyebrows at her interrogatively.

'Of course! It *is* your painting, isn't it?'

'It's mine, but I didn't—'

'Well then! No use prevaricating any more—I've already sent it in!'

He had replaced the receiver irritably and turned to Ailsa. 'Old Anderson came snooping round here this evening, convinced I wasn't serious about not having anything. He seems to have landed on the birthday painting. We might as well let him have it; it'll keep him quiet and you weren't going to enter it yourself, were you?'

Until his memory played back the scene he hadn't realised how arrogant and hurtful the words must have sounded to her: his careless assumption that since obviously it stood no chance of winning the competition, its being entered under the wrong name didn't matter too much. No wonder that from that day on the gulf between them had widened.

'How you must have hated me!' he said in a low voice. 'It's a fantastic picture, haunting somehow. Don't worry, I'll get things straightened out right away and then you'll get all the credit you deserve.'

Her eyes, which had closed wearily during his silence, flickered open. 'No, Jamie, no. What's the use?'

'But of course I must! I can't possibly—'

'Whisht, of course you can! What good would it be to me?'

Appalled, he stared at her. 'Ailsa, what do you mean? Don't talk like that!'

'Keep it, Jamie. Promise—not to say anything. It was always for you anyway. I can't take back a present, can I?'

He pressed her hand fiercely against his cheek, struggling to find the right word to negate her hopelessness, and into the throbbing silence a voice said suddenly, 'Daddy, where am I? What's happening?'

His head jerked up. Ailsa hadn't moved; her eyes were still closed. The voice must have come from the other side of the screen. Poor kid, he thought dispassionately, before his mind swung back to his own pain.

He was still miserably clutching her hand when a gentle touch on his shoulder spun him round to see the nurse behind him.

'Not yet!' he pleaded. 'Please!'

'You've had longer than two minutes. Come along, now, you'll only tire her. She must rest.'

Reluctantly he stood up, releasing from his fingers the limp, flaccid hand. Awkwardly he bent and kissed her forehead. 'I'll come again tomorrow,' he promised in a choked voice. It might have been an attempt at a smile or a mere muscular twitch which moved her lips, but she hadn't the strength to open her eyes again. Perhaps she knew that for her there would be no tomorrow.

In silence the nurse accompanied him as he stumbled back the interminable length of the ward. It crossed his mind that she was afraid he might fall. In any case he was grateful for her implied support. At the door he turned to her beseechingly.

'There is—some hope, isn't there?'

Her eyes were full of compassion and gave the lie to her calm, professional reply. 'There's always hope, laddie. There's always hope.'

CHAPTER ONE

I had never liked the painting, but I'm not sure at what point I actually became afraid of it.

It was this picture which, twenty years ago, had set Lance on the ladder to success, had in fact made his reputation overnight, and it had haunted us all the time we'd been together. It was reproduced on calendars, in glossy magazines, even on biscuit tins and chocolate boxes, and whenever Lance's name was mentioned—in television interviews or the learned art columns of the more erudite Sunday newspapers, it was always with the corollary 'the artist who as a student created such a stir with his brilliant allegorical painting *Eternal Spring*'. And all the time the original hung in pride of place over the sitting-room mantelpiece, beautiful, mystical and somehow full of menace.

Part of my dislike was probably a frustrated

jealousy because of the importance it obviously held for both Lance and Briony. Lance himself seemed to have a love-hate relationship with it. Once, he had even burst out uncharacteristically, 'Good grief, you'd think I'd never painted anything else! Why can't they let it rest in peace and refer to some of the later works?' Often in the evenings I would notice his eyes on it and a look of brooding sadness on his face.

Briony, on the other hand, seemed to regard it more as a private source of energy. Increasingly during the last year or so she had gone straight into the sitting-room on her return from school 'to recharge my batteries from Daddy's picture!' (Lance had been 'Daddy' to her for sixteen of the eighteen years of her life, but to my continual surprise, despite his very obvious devotion to her, he still made a point of introducing her as his step-daughter.)

On reflection now, it seems only too obvious that my emotions regarding the two people whom I loved more than life itself were in a considerable turmoil long before events started to move with the increased momentum which soon threatened to become a headlong rush to disaster. I didn't, of course, admit, even to myself, that the strength of affection between my husband and daughter was another cause of disquiet. Briony had brought us together in the first place, and it seemed more and more obvious that but for her there would have been no question of our marriage. In the early days, blinded by the force of my own love, I had laughingly confessed that I wasn't sure whether it was she or myself whom Lance had married, but for many years now, as our own relationship remained the formal, mildly affectionate one of comparative strangers, it had not seemed funny at all.

It was not that his was an undemonstrative nature, but that all his spontaneous hugs and kisses were reserved solely for Briony. To myself he was unfailingly gentle, kind and considerate, keeping to the letter his original proposal of a marriage of convenience which was also virtually platonic, for the infrequent times he came to my bed he was almost apologetic about it. Sometimes, lying awake far into the night after he had left me, tears drying on my cheeks, I would think resentfully that he used me as he would a woman of the streets—only in moments of extreme need.

In my own mind, I date that increased tempo of events from the May afternoon when I met Jan Staveley by chance in Rushyford and accepted her invitation to join her for a cup of tea. Jan was the mother of Briony's current boyfriend, Mark, and I liked her the best of our large and rather superficial circle of friends. That afternoon, however, she was not meeting my eyes and I waited with sick expectancy for her to tell me what was troubling her. Perhaps I already guessed.

11

We talked lightly of nothing in particular until the waitress had laid in front of us the chrome teapot and butter-soaked scones that Jan, with a rueful pat of her rather ample hips, had been unable to resist. Then, diffidently, she enquired, 'How's Briony? I haven't seen her lately.'

So my guess had been right. I felt my mouth go dry but my voice sounded normal enough as I replied steadily, 'Working hard, of course. The A-levels are looming ever nearer.'

'I hope she isn't—overdoing it.'

I forced myself to look across at her, but her eyes were fixed firmly on her plate. 'What's the matter, Jan?'

She flashed me an apprehensive glance. 'How do you mean?'

'You want to tell me something. What is it? Something to do with Briony?'

'It's only that you said some time ago you were worried about those headaches she was having. Did you ever find out what was causing them?'

I realised I'd been stirring my tea for some minutes and forced myself to lay the spoon down in the saucer. 'Only in so far as there doesn't seem to *be* any cause.'

'The doctor couldn't find anything wrong?'

'No, and he was very thorough. He even arranged for her to go to the hospital for a series of tests and X-rays, but everything proved negative. Her eyesight is perfect and

12

there's no suggestion of any tumour, or epilepsy, or hardening of the arteries supplying the brain, or any of the other horrors I'd hardly dared to think about. All they came up with was "tension"—and I could have told them that myself. She probably is working too hard, as you said, but once the exams are over she'll be all right.'

It was what I had been telling myself for some months and I waited for her reassuring murmur of assent. When it didn't come I persisted, 'Why do you ask? Has Mark said anything?'

Jan flushed guiltily. 'Not really. I probably shouldn't have—'

'Jan, please! I have a right to know. What did he say?'

'Well, it's just that—' She looked up at me, squared her shoulders and went on more firmly, 'As a matter of fact he has been a bit worried about her, yes. He says she acts rather—strangely at times.'

The blood began to beat in my head in an insistent rhythmic pounding. 'How strangely?'

'He calls it—"going away."'

'*Going away?*' My throat ached with the effort of forcing the words out.

Jan hurried on, still not looking at me. 'He says that sometimes when they're together she suddenly—gives herself a little shake, and she's—different, somehow. Even her voice seems to change, he said.'

13

So what I had begun to dread was really happening. I could no longer comfort myself that it was imagination: Mark had noticed it too. My mind shuddered away from the terrifying implications as the familiar palliatives came to my rescue. Briony had always been as changeable as quicksilver. When she was quite small, my mother used to remark that she should be an actress when she grew up. 'I've never seen a face able to change so much from one minute to the next! She might be a completely different person!'

But there was no denying that there had also been occasions over the years when the child had shown an unnervingly accurate precognition. This had always been in regard to very minor instances—the arrival of a letter with a certain item of news, and so on. It was not what she knew but how she knew it which had so alarmed me and probably made me overreact. It was some time now since anything had been said on this subject, but I had the uncomfortable feeling that she probably still had these flashes but had learned to keep them to herself.

I said with an effort, 'Can you give me an example?'

'Well, for as long as we've known her, Briony's always been extremely allergic to shrimps.' I nodded. 'Last Saturday she suddenly insisted on having a whole plateful of them. Nothing Mark said would change her

14

mind, and what's more she ate the lot without any ill effects. Then, oh, about half an hour later, he said she gave this little shiver again and looked up at him and said "How silly, I must have fallen asleep! Have you ordered lunch?"'

I could feel my heart beating high in my chest with a vehemence that made me feel slightly sick. It was worse, very much worse, than I'd realised. 'How often has this kind of thing happened?'

'Only a couple of times. Three at the most, I'd say. Mark came to me because he was afraid of the responsibility of keeping it to himself any longer. I said I'd mention it to you.'

'Thank you,' I said aridly.

'He might be exaggerating, of course. Perhaps it wasn't as obvious as it sounds. I mean, no one else seemed to notice anything. She was quite—rational.'

'Just different.'

'Yes.' Jan moved uncomfortably. 'I hope I did the right thing in telling you.'

'It couldn't have been a coma?'

'I don't think so. She was talking and everything.'

'But she didn't remember anything when she "came back"?'

Jan shook her head wordlessly.

'Oh God!' I said in a whisper.

'But you say she's been thoroughly examined. There can't be much wrong, surely,

15

or they'd have discovered it.'

'Perhaps. Jan—' I licked paper-dry lips, tried to marshal some sort of order out of the chaos of my thoughts. 'Don't say anything to anyone else, will you?'

'Oh Ann, of *course* not! You *know*—'

'I mean—actually, I mean especially to Lance.'

She looked surprised but merely answered, 'I wouldn't think of it.'

'It's just that—well, you know how he is about her, and if any little thing is wrong he panics immediately. That might be bad for her.'

'Yes, I see what you mean.'

'Also, he's working very hard at the moment to complete this collection for the exhibition next month. I don't want him to have any additional worries.'

'Ann—forgive me for asking, but I was wondering: does Briony remember her real father?'

I stared at her in bewilderment, trying to adjust to what seemed an entirely new topic. 'I shouldn't think so. She was only six months old when he was killed. Why?'

'It's just that psychiatrists and people like that always seem to look for an explanation in childhood, don't they, for any kind of— disturbance? I wondered if she was old enough to have missed him.'

I smiled slightly. 'I doubt it. Any other

16

theories, Mrs Freud?'

Jan flushed but persisted doggedly. 'She might have resented Lance at first? After all, for—what, a year?—there had just been the two of you.'

I shook my head decidedly. 'No, no, positively and emphatically no. Far from being left out, she was the one Lance noticed in the first place.' I gave a little laugh that didn't quite come off, and bit my lip.

'I don't remember hearing how you met.'

'We were on holiday in Scotland, Mother, Briony and I. It was the year after Michael was killed—Briony would have been about eighteen months old.'

'How terrible to have been left like that with a young baby. You were hardly more than a child yourself.'

I hesitated. 'Actually, Jan, you might as well know the truth. It hadn't been a happy marriage.' After nineteen years I had actually said it aloud. 'I knew almost at once it was a mistake,' I went on more slowly. 'He was gay and handsome and ten years older than I was, but he drank too much even then and it got steadily worse. There were nights when he didn't come home at all and I'd lie awake waiting for some hospital to ring. There were probably faults on both sides; I dare say I didn't turn out the way he expected, either. Anyway, when he was killed in that crash—he was drunk, of course—I—well, I grieved for

17

the waste of it all, but—it sounds terrible put into words, but I certainly wasn't heartbroken.'

Jan leant forward and put her square, dimpled little hand gently over mine. 'I'm sorry. I didn't mean to pry.'

'It's all right.' But I found I couldn't go on to tell her about meeting Lance after all. Quite suddenly I had to be alone, away from her sympathetic eyes and gentle questioning. 'Actually I'll have to go. Briony'll be home any minute. Thanks for the tea.'

I was thankful that she had the tact not to accompany me. Out in the narrow street the sun was still shining, and the fact that it stung my eyes made me realise the strain I'd been under for the last half hour. I almost ran to the car park, fumbling in my bag for the keys. The streets were filling now with newly-released school children, the girls swinging their panama hats, their dresses splashes of colour against the mellow stone, and the boys teetering slowly alongside on their bicycles. I couldn't see Briony among them. I inched the car into the stream of traffic clogging the narrow roads and made my way slowly up out of the busy little market town into the rolling peace of the Suffolk countryside.

In the driving mirror my cheeks looked flushed and the little network of fine lines I'd only recently noticed at the corners of my eyes seemed more apparent. Impatiently I would

18

down the window and let the welcome breeze lift my hair. Friday afternoon; the weekend lay ahead. No doubt the usual crowd would converge on us on Sunday.

Subconsciously my foot pressed the accelerator and the little car leapt forward, startling a pheasant which rose from the side of the road in an extravagant display of colour. How lovely everything was: the pastel colours of the farmhouses, sky blue, apricot and yellow, the clumps of trees straight from a Constable landscape. If only I were free to revel in it, to enjoy it all as it should be enjoyed, without that eternal rider 'if only'. If only Lance loved me; if only Briony could outgrow this strangeness; if only we could sometimes be alone together without having to fill the house with people.

The painted white gates of Fairfield Lodge came into sight and I turned into them, thankful to escape from my disquieting thoughts. The old house looked at its most beautiful in the afternoon sunshine and as always my heart lifted at the sight of it. The garage doors stood open and a bicycle leaned drunkenly against the wall. Briony was home. I pushed open the front door and the sunshine followed me inside. At the end of the hall the kitchen door opened and Mrs Rose appeared.

'The kettle's on, Mrs Tenby, if you're ready for your tea.'

'I've just had some, thanks. Have you taken

my husband his?'

'Not yet; I'm getting it now.'

'Let me know when it's ready and I'll take it myself. Is Miss Briony upstairs?'

'I think she went into the sitting-room, ma'am.'

My heart sank, and I pushed the door open. Sure enough, Briony had flung herself on to the sofa and was leaning back gazing up at the painting over the mantelpiece. Resentfully I stood in the doorway and let my own eyes be drawn by the magnetism of it. The scene was an enchanted garden, full of birds and spring flowers, an Arcadian paradise. Beneath a cherry tree laden with blossom two lovers stood hand in hand, eternally young. But beyond the garden walls winter had come. The skies were hard and grey, the trees skeletal in their nakedness and, most horrible of all, a group of bent, aged figures, gaunt-eyed and grey-haired, gazed with bitter longing at the inaccessible promise of the garden.

As always a shiver snaked down my spine and I must have made some movement because Briony turned, her face still blank with the intensity of her absorption. Then she smiled and sat up. 'Hello, I didn't hear the car.'

I had driven right past the window; she should have heard it. I said lightly, 'I presume you haven't been in long? Rushyford's still moving with your fellow scholars.'

'Only five minutes or so. Rosie's bringing me

20

a cup of tea when she's made Daddy's.'

'You're looking tired, darling.' I tried to keep the anxiety out of my voice. 'You've not had another of your headaches, have you?'

'No, not today. Do you know, Mother, I've just been thinking I'd rather like to do a bit of painting myself.'

I stared at her in surprise. 'My dear child, you can't even draw a straight line!'

'That's no reason why I shouldn't start now. Look at Grandma Moses! Oh, not till after A's of course, but it would be something to do when all the studying's over.' She glanced at me and gave a little laugh. 'You know, it was rather odd. I was looking at the painting a minute ago, and I suddenly thought, "It's far and away the best thing I've done"! Wasn't that strange, as if I'd painted it myself?'

I said evenly, 'Actually I'm glad you didn't. I've never liked that picture very much.'

'Really? Why ever not?'

'I don't know. It depresses me, all those poor souls shut outside and the uncaring lovers in the garden. It seems—egotistical, somehow.'

'Because Daddy is one of the lovers?'

My eyes went quickly to her innocently questioning face. 'I don't know,' I answered slowly. 'That hadn't struck me before.'

'I'd always somehow assumed that he was.'

Perhaps, I thought painfully, my fear and dislike had no more basis than that. Nothing sinister after all, merely subconscious

21

resentment of Lance in that lyrical garden with—someone else. Now that I looked more closely, the male figure certainly had fair hair.

I said quickly, 'Whatever the reason, I've never liked it, though I realise I'm in a minority of one. It's just bad luck that it happens to be my wall that it hangs on! I'm always hoping Daddy'll accept one of these astronomical offers people keep making for it. Think what we'd save in insurance premiums!'

Behind me Mrs Rose said, 'Here's the master's tea, ma'am' and I took the tray out of her hands. 'Yours is in the kitchen, Miss Briony.'

'Thanks, Rosie. I'll come and have it now.'

I went through the open french windows and down the terrace steps. The shadows lay across the grass, subtly altering its shades of green. I had become very colour-conscious since Lance came into my life.

The studio had originally been the stable block and was screened from the house by a high bank of sweet-smelling shrubs. Its modernisation had included washing facilities and an electric hob for making tea or even boiling eggs if Lance didn't want the interruption of returning to the house for meals. Double-glazed windows ran the length of two walls, but in today's sunshine he had flung them open and was at his easel with his shirt unbuttoned to the waist.

He looked up at my approach and smiled.

'That looks good. Thank you. I'd no idea of the time. Is Briony home?'

'Yes. She's just had her usual meditation in front of the painting.' I felt him glance at me sharply but kept my eyes on the tray as I bent down and put it on the table beside him.

'How's the magnum opus?'

'Oh—' He ran a hand through his thick hair. 'Not so bad, I suppose. I still break out in a cold sweat when I remember there are three more to do before the end of June. By the way, are the Pomfretts coming on Sunday?'

'I imagine so. Why?'

'I'd like a word with Stella. It's just a vague idea at the moment, but I think I could work her into a painting. Do you think she'd let me try?'

'I imagine she'd jump at it,' I returned drily. 'Most people have to pay through the nose for the privilege!'

'It wouldn't be strictly a portrait, more a— representation, but I've often thought I'd like to capture her on canvas. She has a lovely face and perfect bone structure, but it's that superb colouring I'm after.'

'I never knew you cared!' I said with brittle flippancy.

He laughed. 'Don't worry, it's professional interest only. She's not my type.'

But nor am I, I thought achingly. And whether Stella was his type or not, I didn't doubt that he was hers. Like most of my

23

women friends, she played up to him almost unconsciously. I really couldn't blame her. Lance must seem a romantic figure to them, tall and fair with steady, deep-set grey eyes and his slow smile, quite apart from the added ingredient of his considerable fame as an artist. I was fully aware of the envy I aroused. They weren't to know that my own relationship with him was scarcely more intimate than theirs. I for my part passionately envied Stella the prospect of long hours ahead in this sweet-smelling seclusion with Lance.

'What do you want her to represent?'

'I'm not sure exactly. Woman through the ages type of thing—the eternal female—earth mother. Anyway, I'll see what she says. Oh, and before I forget, I met rather a pleasant chap at the golf club yesterday. Forrest, his name was. I told him if he and his family would like to come along on Sunday we'd be pleased to see them. They haven't been here long and don't know many people.'

'How many children has he?'

'Twin daughters, I believe. Briony probably knows them, they'll be about her age.'

'So that's the Pomfretts and ourselves—seven—and this new crowd, eleven—and Cynthia and Edgar are bound to come—thirteen, and of course Mark.'

Lance frowned and drained his cup. 'I'm not too keen on Briony seeing quite so much of that young man.'

24

I smiled wryly. 'And what's wrong with this one?'

He met my eyes defensively. 'What do you mean?'

'Oh come on, Lance! You know you find faults with all of them. The fact is you don't like Briony seeing much of *anyone* except—' Somehow I managed to swallow back 'you' and substitute 'us'.

'She's too young to be tied up with boys,' he said stubbornly.

'She's nearly eighteen. What do you expect?' For the first time the thought flashed through my head: what will happen when Briony eventually gets married? Will our own marriage be able to withstand her loss, or will it simply crumble away to nothing? I looked down at Lance's tanned slightly frowning face in sudden fear. Almost academically I wondered what his reaction would be if I took his head between my hands and kissed him hard on the mouth. Embarrassed surprise, probably. As far as he was concerned, our marriage was what he had always intended it to be—a pleasant enough way of keeping Briony at his side. In all fairness he had never pretended otherwise.

I gave my head a quick little shake, picked up the empty cup and left him. He did not try to detain me. Across the garden the house stood waiting, gracious and dignified. As I regained the height of the terrace I could see over the

25

stone wall which surrounded the pool and its sunbathing area, and caught sight of Dick, the younger gardener, busy with the filters. Fleetingly I wondered whether to have a swim before dinner and decided against it.

Averting my eyes from the painting, I went swiftly back through the sitting-room to return the tray to Mrs Rose.

CHAPTER TWO

I didn't sleep well that night. Worries which could be forced beneath the surface during daylight hours emerged to fill my head with their buzzing possibilities. For some reason that I couldn't even begin to define, Briony's casual remark that she would like to take up painting, which at the time I'd hardly considered, loomed large among them. Jealousy again, I told myself in exasperation. It was another thread which would draw her and Lance closer together and as such I resented it. But I couldn't dismiss it as easily as that. The whole world of art seemed full of menace where it touched Briony—and that line of thought clearly stemmed from her obsession with the painting downstairs. In my feverish imagination it seemed to be endowed with some evil power of its own, luring her ever closer like an obscene carnivorous plant until it could digest her as an integral part of itself.

I sat up suddenly and switched on the light. The familiar outlines of the bedroom leapt reassuringly at me out of the darkness. In the next bed Lance lay breathing gently, his face in sleep younger and more vulnerable than the daylight world was allowed to see it. For several minutes I stared across at him, waiting for my chaotic breathing to quieten. He knew, of course, about Briony's headaches, but the less tangible fears I had kept to myself. For the next few weeks, while he was working at full stretch to fulfil the exhibition requirements as well as keeping up his three day week lecturing at the local art college, I didn't want to add to his worries. And far from acting as a calming influence on me, where Briony was concerned he was apt to panic even more than I was. It was therefore impossible to tell him Jan's disquieting words about her 'going away', about her sudden seeming immunity to a previously powerful allergy. With a sigh I reached up and switched off the light, watching my husband's face vanish again into the dark.

Sleep came, but only fitfully, and at breakfast I was still tired and tense. The morning sunshine flooded through the open dining-room windows, glinting blindingly on the cut-glass marmalade dish and the flashing silver of Briony's spoon as she ate her grapefruit. Across the table Lance emerged from his newspaper and smiled at her. 'We've

27

that tennis match to finish this afternoon, haven't we? I seem to remember we had to abandon it at my leading five-three in the third set.'

'Oh Daddy, I can't this afternoon, I'm afraid.'

'But it was all arranged,' I said quickly, seeing the disappointment on Lance's face. 'You know how Daddy enjoys your Saturday tennis. It's about the only relaxation he gets.'

'I'm sorry, I simply forgot all about it. Mark told me yesterday that there's a pop group appearing in Marshford tonight. We thought we'd walk there, having a picnic lunch on the way, and catch the last bus home. We can play tomorrow instead.'

'The crowd will be here tomorrow,' Lance said quietly. 'Never mind, obviously Mark has first refusal. But where in Marshford can they possibly hold a concert?'

'The Congregational Hall. Mark managed to get almost the last two tickets.'

'Good for him.'

The sour note in his voice must have reached her, for she stretched out impulsively for his hand. 'Daddy darling, I do believe you're jealous! You needn't be, you know, ever. I'll always love you best!'

The breath twisted in my throat. Since my eyes were on his face I caught for a split second his startled acceptance of her accusation before he recovered himself and smilingly patted her hand.

'I'll go and see what Rosie's rustled up for the picnic.' She pushed her chair back from the table and left the room. I said carefully into the silence, 'I'll have a game with you this afternoon if you like.'

'What?' He brought his eyes back to me with an effort.

'I said—'

'Oh. No, it's all right. I should be working anyway.' He wiped his mouth slowly with his napkin. 'You know, she could be right. I'm in danger of becoming possessive and that's bad. You said the same thing yourself, didn't you?'

'She has to grow away from us a little,' I said painfully.

'I suppose so, yes.'

With a glance at his face I changed the subject. 'I suppose you're doing your coaching this morning as usual. How's it coming along?'

'Surprisingly well, now. It was really only started as a kind of therapy, you know—something Paul could do even if he'd never walk again. But we seem to have touched on a hidden talent, and he's far better than ever I or his parents expected.'

'Perhaps some good will come out of that ghastly accident after all. All the same, it's a pity it takes up all your Saturday mornings.'

He glanced at his watch. 'I must be going. See you at lunch time.' He hesitated. 'You will make sure Briony takes sensible things if she's

29

to be out all day? A hat, for instance. The sun will be pretty fierce today and we don't want any more of those headaches. And a jacket or something for coming home. It's still early enough in the year to be cool at night.'

'I'll check, but she's pretty sensible.'

'Yes.' He smiled vaguely and went out. Shakily I put my hands to my head. Was I imagining all these subtle undertones? On the surface it had been a normal enough breakfast, but to my finely tuned nerves it seemed that yet another small, insignificant landmark had been passed along the road to—what? And when would we reach the point of no return?

Briony swished back and dropped on to her chair. 'Any coffee left?'

'A little, I think.' I drained the pot carefully into her outstretched cup.

She eyed me uncertainly. 'Daddy didn't mind too much about the tennis, did he?'

'Not enough to take up my offer as a substitute, anyway! But you do owe him a bit of consideration, you know, and it wouldn't hurt Mark to learn that you aren't ready to drop everything to fit in with his suggestions.'

She dimpled. 'No, Mother! Point taken.'

'He told me to make sure you take a sunhat and a jacket for coming home.'

'Bless him,' she said complacently. I looked across at her, trying not to resent her casual acceptance of his love. Almost absentmindedly she reached out for the last piece of toast in the rack and began to butter it. 'Has he asked Mrs Pomfrett to sit for him yet?' she enquired with her mouth full.

'How did you know about that?'

'He mentioned it a week or two ago, when we were discussing the range of pictures for the exhibition.' I was silent. He hadn't discussed it with me. 'He'll probably ask her tomorrow,' she added. 'I wonder if he'll do her in the nude.'

That possibility had not occurred to me. Lance's nudes were few and far between—but an earth mother? It was possible. Briony said with a giggle, 'She mightn't let him. She's probably a bit flabby without her girdle!'

I said severely, '*Mr* Pomfrett mightn't let him. And don't be disrespectful about your parents' friends!'

'Well really Mother, she is a bit heavy round the hips. And even if she has got gorgeous features and wonderful colouring, she hasn't much about her, has she? She reminds me of a beautiful doll. Come to think of it, Mr's a bit too good to be true, too, with those perfect teeth and all that dark hair. They make what Granny used to call a striking pair!'

My mind flickered to Simon Pomfrett, aptly summed up, I had to admit, by my daughter.

'Their children are much more human,' she continued. 'Lindsay's hair is just fair, not that rich gold, and Roger's dark without being blue-black—kind of watered down and not so perfect. I suppose they'll be coming tomorrow.

31

They can make up a foursome with Mark and me.'

Belatedly I remembered the extra guests Lance had invited. 'Do you know any girls at school called Forrest? Twins, I think.'

'Rachel and Rebecca? Yes, they're new this term.'

'Daddy's invited them and their family tomorrow too.'

'Well, they're pleasant enough, but they'll foul up the tennis four. It's going to be quite a crowd, isn't it? I suppose the Pembertons will be here too?'

'Probably.'

'You know, I think old Edgar rather fancies you!'

'Briony!'

'Well, I do! He's always watching you. And heaven knows he can't have much of a life with her!'

'Now really—' I began helplessly, and she gave a bubble of unrepentant laughter.

'Don't try to look shocked, Mother. You know quite well what I mean! I can't stand that woman and I bet you can't, either. Why we have to suffer her every weekend, just so Daddy can play host to the district, I don't know.'

'That's quite enough,' I said firmly, standing up.

She finished her coffee. 'Well, I do get a bit sick of these social occasions. Once or twice

32

would be fine, but not *every* weekend. We never carried on like this when Granny was alive.'

No, I thought reflectively, while Mother was still here we weren't such a compact unit. Once she'd gone we shrank to a normal two-generation family with its increased intimacy, and Lance didn't want that. There could be no other explanation for his careful arranging of Saturday morning coaching and open house every Sunday. And without Briony to play tennis this afternoon, he would rapidly retreat to the studio. Did I really bore him that much?

'Oh well, I'd better do an hour's German before Mark comes.'

I made some automatic reply as she left the room, but memories of my meeting with Lance, jolted yesterday by Jan's questioning, were flooding back into my mind and this time I let them come: the quiet little hotel out among the heather, the blue smudge of the hills, the lochs and the seabirds and the wild, singing loneliness.

It struck me suddenly that even though she had been so tiny, Scotland had apparently made a deep impression on Briony, too—perhaps because we had met Lance there. I couldn't think of any other explanation for her passionate interest in all things Scottish, the books she collected on its history, the formation of ancient clans and tartans, even the classics by Scott and Stevenson which I myself had always found heavy. And yet there had been that curious reaction earlier this year when, thinking to please her, I'd suggested we might go back for a holiday. 'No!' she'd exclaimed breathlessly. 'Please don't make me! I can't!'

I had stared at her with complete incomprehension. 'But darling, I thought you'd love it! Why ever don't you want to go?'

'I just don't.' She'd calmed down when she realised I was not insisting, and then she added, almost to herself, 'Anyway, it isn't time yet.'

Once again I helplessly abandoned the attempt to understand my daughter and my mind returned to that first holiday. I had noticed Lance at once, solitary and withdrawn across the dining-room, and as the days passed I found myself looking out for him, attempting a shy smile which was never reciprocated, watching wistfully from the window as he strode out, always alone, across the moors.

Just as I had resigned myself to never coming to his notice, Briony took matters into her own hands. Being still at the messy stage, she didn't eat with the rest of the guests, and one evening I was later than usual giving her her tea. Our table was near the door of the dining-room, and Lance came through the hall. Immediately a wide smile spread over her face and she shouted gleefully, 'Dad-dad!'

I still don't know where she had learnt the word. Lance turned, of course, and I was covered with confusion, murmuring incoherent apologies. I needn't have bothered. He came slowly into the room and stood staring down at her and as I watched anxiously, his face, so bleak and withdrawn, seemed to soften and become vulnerable again. And that was it. Love at first sight, for both of them.

With shaking hands, my thoughts still rooted in the past, I began to stack the breakfast plates. From then on, he just wanted to be with her. It was as simple as that. I was accepted tacitly as a necessary appendage, someone to help manoeuvre the pushchair over the uneven ground, someone to cope when she succumbed to hiccups. And at the end of the fortnight he couldn't let her go.

After dinner that last evening he asked me to go for a walk. It was the first time that Briony hadn't been with us. He was very calm and matter-of-fact. He said we had both lost the only person who would ever mean anything to us—I didn't contradict him—but that it was no reason why we should have to spend the rest of our lives alone. He said he didn't like to think of me having all the responsibility of looking after Briony and Mother as well. (She was a semi-invalid even then.) He was quite frank about not having intended to marry, but he now found he was fond of children, and Briony obviously needed a father. For the rest, he had good prospects and could offer me a pleasant home, together with the staff to run it smoothly and without effort. I was left with the impression that all that was required of me in return was to supervise the household and be a pleasant hostess to his friends.

I didn't, of course, realise then who he was, though he was already well-known in art circles. It was all very civilised and reasonable and might indeed have been as convenient as he imagined but for one factor. I could hardly explain that my own feelings for Michael had simply been schoolgirl infatuation and that, as I knew even then, Lance himself was to be the great love of my life. By the same token, I could not summon up the courage to ask him about the girl he had loved and lost, and he never mentioned her again.

I came back to the present with the awareness of slow tears of self-pity brimming in my eyes and impatiently pulled myself together. However it had come about, I was married to the man I loved. I had a great deal for which to be thankful.

Mark called for Briony about eleven o'clock and I spent the rest of the morning with Mrs Rose discussing catering arrangements for the next day. Lance and I had a light lunch under the sun umbrella on the terrace. Beyond, the garden stretched freshly green and immaculate. The air was full of birdsong and on the fruit trees at the end of the garden the last of the blossom still clung, curly brown and dry, between the tender new leaves.

Unable to let well alone, I said out of the blue, 'Has Briony mentioned that she's thinking of taking up painting?'

I wasn't sure if I had imagined his moment of complete immobility. He said carefully, 'No, she hasn't. When did she reach that momentous decision?'

'Yesterday, I believe. Under the influence of *Eternal Spring*.'

He moistened his lips. 'But she's all geared towards languages now.'

'For the exams, yes, but only because she had to choose something. She's never had any idea what she wanted to do. Perhaps all your early tuition's paid off after all. Remember trailing her round the galleries when she could scarcely walk, and the inevitable paintbox in her Christmas stocking?'

He smiled slightly but his face looked strained. 'I don't think she ever even opened them. I found three or four of them once, at the back of the toy cupboard, still looking brand new. Of course, there was no real reason to think she'd be interested. It's not as though it could be hereditary, after all.' The old, inexplicable insistence on no blood ties.

'Environment, then,' I suggested lightly. 'I presume you wouldn't object if she was serious about it?'

'Object? I couldn't be more delighted, but it would mean damned hard work, coming to it

37

cold as it were.'

'Paul Beddowes did.'

'True.'

'Would you teach her yourself?'

He hesitated. 'A little, perhaps, but someone less involved would probably be better for her. Anyway, we mustn't get too carried away with all this. If it was just a casual remark she may have forgotten all about it.'

I looked at him quickly, but there seemed to be no hidden meaning in his suggestion of her forgetfulness. Perhaps, if he'd noticed it at all, he merely accepted it as a normal part of her character. And perhaps it was.

I said abruptly, 'I had tea with Jan in Rushyford yesterday. She was asking how we first met. It was strange, thinking back over it all.'

His face softened. 'Briony in her high chair, with jam all over her face!'

Not a word about me and our coolly rational agreement.

Mrs Rose was already hovering to collect the dishes. Her Saturday afternoons were free and she usually managed to catch the two o'clock bus from the stop a hundred yards down the road. Reluctantly, since prolonging the conversation would be of no avail, I nodded to her to begin to clear. Lance stood up and stretched. 'Well, back to work. See you later.' And he strolled down the steps and across the grass to the studio.

I was hot and sticky in my blouse and skirt and went upstairs to change into a cotton sundress. A new library book lay on the bedside table. I picked it up, found my dark glasses and went back outside.

Dick Gifford had set up a couple of deck chairs on the lawn before he went home at lunch time. I carried one of them down the shallow steps of the sunken rose garden. Saturday afternoon and alone as usual. I lay back and closed my eyes, hopeful of reclaiming some of the previous night's lost sleep, but almost at once the click of the side gate roused me. Mrs Rose had already left and the gardeners had finished work for the weekend.

I sat up, shading my eyes, in time to see Edgar Pemberton come round the corner of the terrace wall. He raised a hand when he saw me and started to come over. 'I think he rather fancies you' had vouchsafed my disrespectful daughter. For the first time I considered her words, weighing them in my mind as he approached. I had to concede it was possible.

Edgar and Cynthia lived further out along the Stowmarket road and he frequently dropped in as he was passing with some fruit he had happened to see at a green-grocer's, with an art catalogue that might interest Lance, or just for a cup of tea and a chat. As Briony had shrewdly remarked, there was not much comfort for him at home, and I had perhaps gone out of my way to make him welcome at the Lodge. If that had been the impetus for his revised assessment of me, I should have to be careful. But I *liked* Edgar, I thought with a hint of defiance. His kind, unassuming friendliness did a great deal to compensate for his wife's barbed witticisms.

'Not disturbing you, am I?' he called as he came up.

'No, I'm delighted to have someone to talk to! Bring that other chair and join me for a while.'

I noticed that he was carrying a shallow wooden seed box and he set it on the ground between us while he put up the deck chair. 'I brought you some of those cuttings you said you'd like.'

'Oh, bless you! I'd forgotten about them. Thank you.'

'Briony out?'

'Yes, she and Mark are walking to Marshford, if you please, to a pop concert or something.'

'It seems quite a thing with those two.'

'For the moment, yes.'

'And no doubt Leonardo's closeted in his studio?'

I smiled. 'Time and exhibitions wait for no man.'

'You must spend a lot of time by yourself. Doesn't it worry you?'

'Unfortunately five-day weeks and overtime bans don't apply to artists. I knew that when I

40

married him, so I can't complain.'

'All the same, Cynthia'd never put up with it.' He lay back in the chair and closed his eyes. 'Gosh, this is quite a sun-trap, isn't it?'

Musingly I looked across at him. There were beads of perspiration on his forehead and the dark hair was definitely receding. His neck and jawline had thickened over the years and the darkness of his jowls unfairly made him appear in need of a shave. Poor Edgar, he had not worn as well as Lance, and Cynthia would have resented his unguarded submission to my scrutiny. For myself, I found it oddly touching. I settled back again and closed my eyes, content to have his undemanding company. When I opened them again some time later, it was to find him in his turn studying me and, with Briony's words still fresh in my mind, my heart gave an awkward little jerk. He smiled as our eyes met but made no attempt to look away, and the resulting long-held glance somehow assumed an added importance. To end what was in danger of becoming embarrassing—Edgar, for goodness sake!—I said lazily, 'I'm just trying to work up enough energy to go in search of lemonade.'

'Shall I call Mrs Rose for you?'

'No good, I'm afraid, it's her afternoon off. There's no help for it, I'll have to get it myself.'

'Can't I see to it?'

'No, you don't know where everything is. Don't encourage me to be so idle!' I stood up

41

and pulled down my sundress. The cotton was sticking to the small of my back and I could feel my hair curling closely in the nape of my neck.

'At least I'll come and carry it out for you. What about Lance? Will he join us?'

'I'll take his glass to the studio.'

We walked up the shallow steps, over the hot grass and round the terrace to the kitchen door at the side of the house. Sunless in the afternoons, the air struck cool to our heated bodies. For the first time in my life I was acutely aware of Edgar, and I also knew that he intended me to be. I was not sure whether to be amused or annoyed. I took the bottle of home-made lemonade from the fridge, poured it into a crystal jug and filled the jug with chunks of ice which stung my fingers. As I moved round the room I knew that his eyes followed me, and against my will I felt a spark of gratification.

I set the jug down beside the three glasses and Edgar took the tray from me, his fingers brushing against mine—accidentally, of course, I assured myself hurriedly, amazed at how quickly I seemed to have accepted the new position. Yet after all, what had happened? I had surprised him watching me, and he had not looked away! That was literally all there was. If Briony hadn't mentioned her suspicions that morning I would have thought nothing of it.

I led the way back to the garden, trying not to walk self-consciously. Edgar, of all people! I *must* be imagining things. I was behaving like a pathetic, frustrated—My thoughts veered abruptly away from dangerous ground.

'I'll take Lance his drink.'

He had flung open all the windows and was stripped to the waist.

'Refreshment,' I announced lightly. 'Edgar's here. Could you come and join us for a few minutes?'

'Sorry, not at the moment. I've just mixed this umber and I want to use it quickly. Lordie, that's cold.' He set the glass down again. 'What did Edgar want?'

'He brought some cuttings he'd promised.'

'Better keep them in the shade, then, till Jack gets here on Monday.'

'Yes, I will.'

He leant forward to retrieve his brush, the muscles rippling under the brown skin. I turned abruptly and left him. Edgar's attentions, imagined or not, were giving me ideas which were better kept securely buried.

Any rapport that might have been blossoming between us had wilted during my brief absence with Lance. After a few minutes of desultory conversation, Edgar rose to go.

'Thanks again for the cuttings,' I said formally.

'A pleasure. Thanks for the drink. See you tomorrow.'

'Yes.' Thoughtfully I watched him amble slowly away across the garden. Then, with a

43

self-ridiculing smile, I bent to retrieve my library book.

CHAPTER THREE

Late Sunday morning, and behind my protective dark glasses my less than welcoming gaze moved slowly over our guests, spread out in varying forms of undress on the concrete round the pool. In the water the Forrest twins, alike as two peas, floated on their backs, their pale brown hair streaming behind them. Their parents, informally introduced as Max and Paula, were engaged in idle conversation with the Pembertons. I studied them dispassionately. Max was stocky and dark, his bare torso olive-brown and covered with a mat of black curly hair. I noted that his penetrating black eyes seemed to miss nothing, and wondered what his profession was.

His wife had very short, very straight hair which probably cost a fortune in the cutting. Her swimsuit revealed the almost painful thinness of her long body and she had an oddly attractive mannerism of screwing up her large eyes as though she had difficulty in focusing them. Her nails were long and painted bright red and she smoked incessantly, using a jade cigarette holder. Above her head Cynthia's eyes met mine with a humorously interrogative lift of her eyebrows, and I hastily looked away.

Mark and Briony were lying on their stomachs, their heads together. Briony's hair was drying in the sun and with it cascading down her back she reminded me of a mermaid left behind by the tide. I longed to ask Mark how their day had gone yesterday, whether there had been any more unexplained 'absences'. I already tacitly acknowledged that it was no use asking Briony.

Lance had just squatted down beside Stella's deck chair and was topping up her glass from the crystal jug. From her sudden pleased flush, which I was interested to note spread down below the top of her bikini, I guessed he was asking her to sit for him.

It was time to check up on lunch. I put my glass down in the shade and made my way carefully round the edge of the pool to the wrought iron gate with which we attempted to keep neighbouring cats and dogs from the water. Max Forrest punctiliously opened it for me with an odd little bow. He might well have some mid-European blood in him, I reflected—'Forrest' was probably an Anglisization.

As I reached the terrace steps Mrs Rose came out with platters of cold chicken and ham and bowls of crisp salad. Mentally I checked the long table: butter, cheese, French bread, pickles, salad cream, mustard, cutlery wrapped in paper napkins, piles of fruit heaped in bowls at the back.

'Ready, Ann?' Lance called from the pool gate.

'Ready,' I affirmed. One by one the guests began to drift over, serve themselves and retire with laden plates to the groups of chairs on the grass or at the far end of the terrace.

'Can I get you anything?' It was Edgar.

'I'm never very hungry in the heat, thank you.'

'Nor am I.' His smile was gentle and encouraging and I smiled back, ruefully deciding he would make a good animal trainer. He had sensed my frightened withdrawal yesterday and was patiently setting himself to regain my confidence. With a burst of uncharacteristic recklessness, I decided to let him. It was pleasant to be looked at again as though I were a woman.

'Ann!' Stella came up, picking daintily at the food on her plate. 'Did Lance tell you—he wants to paint me! I'm completely shattered!'

'Shattered or flattered?' Edgar asked unexpectedly. Stella glanced at him in surprise.

'Well, both, I suppose.'

'But you agreed?' I asked smoothly.

'Of course I did. I could hardly refuse, could I?' She looked so smug that I had an inhospitable urge to slap her. Nor did Edgar's next query help.

'Has he ever painted you, Ann?'

'No,' I replied caustically. 'I'm strictly the utilitarian model!'

46

His smiling glance went past me and almost imperceptibly hardened. Turning, I saw Lance and Cynthia coming across the grass. In the clear sunlight Cynthia's charms seemed artificial and contrived. Her silver-blonde hair coiled as immaculately as ever in its gleaming chignon, making no concession to her informal dress, and her eyebrows seemed a little too finely plucked, her blue eyes a little too hard. I sensed Edgar's wariness and tempered it with my own assessment of her. She was amusing—usually at someone's else's expense—and undeniably good company. Also, from time to time, as I knew from personal experience, she was capable of an instinctive gesture of kindness or generosity which completely took one by surprise. If only she wouldn't continually belittle her husband, we might all have liked her more and felt less embarrassed in her presence.

Seeing Simon Pomfrett temporarily alone, I moved towards him like the good hostess Lance expected. He smiled at me, his too-perfect teeth flashing in his bronze face. A striking pair, Briony had called them, and it was as a pair that I always thought of the Pomfretts. Simon and Stella complemented each other to such an extent that individually each of them seemed incomplete, only a half of the whole.

'I hear Stella's about to achieve immortality!' he commented as I stopped

47

beside him.

'Or immorality!' came Cynthia's clear, teasing voice. She and Lance were coming up the steps behind us.

'No such luck!' Lance answered with an easy laugh. 'I can't afford to become emotionally involved with my models.'

'Then never paint me, will you darling?' Cynthia moved off in search of food, hips swaying. Lance's amused glance followed her, devoid of interest. At least I needn't fear his infidelity, I reflected morosely. He might hint that involvement would be unwise but I knew instinctively that there was no temptation. Lance had a rigidly strict code of ethics; it would simply not occur to him to be unfaithful to me. A sudden thought struck me like a douche of cold water. Perhaps he even regarded his times with me, reduced as they were to a minimum, as a form of infidelity to the girl whose memory he still so obviously cherished.

'You've no objection to my painting Stella, have you, Simon?' he was asking casually, helping himself to a stick of celery from the plate which Briony was carrying.

'On the contrary—I shall bask in reflected glory!'

Briony removed Lance's glass from his hand, took a sip from it and wrinkled her nose. 'That's vile! Whatever is it?'

'Arsenic laced with belladonna, and no one

48

asked for your opinion.' Almost without thinking he put an arm round her and pulled her against his side for a moment before, with a dismissive little pat, he sent her on her way. That, I thought with the familiar sinking of heart, was the only rival I had to fear, and I was powerless to defend myself and my love against my own daughter.

I turned away to find, rather to my consternation, that the alert black eyes of Max Forrest had witnessed the little incident, including apparently my own reaction to it. Smoothly and with a smile he moved towards me.

'It was very kind of your husband to invite us along today.'

'Not at all. He mentioned that you don't know many people in the district.'

'No, we only moved out here at Easter.'

'Where did you come from?'

'Oh, not far, only Bury St Edmunds. I still have my consulting rooms there.'

I glanced at him quickly. 'Consulting rooms? You're a doctor?'

He smiled. 'Of a kind. A psychiatrist, actually.'

'I see.' I couldn't think of anything else to say, but a host of thoughts chased each other round my head. Could this squat little man be the answer to my prayers—a discreet, sympathetic and at the same time qualified ear into which to pour my flood of anxiety? And

49

yet—to consult a psychiatrist seemed such a positive step, a definite admission that something was seriously wrong.

'You look a little apprehensive, Mrs Tenby!'

'It's only that I've never met a psychiatrist before. I feel I'll have to watch my step!'

He smiled but his attention had shifted to where Briony had joined his daughters on the lawn. I turned to follow his gaze, leaning beside him on the balustrade.

'Your daughter doesn't really resemble either you or your husband,' he remarked with deceptive lightness.

I said tightly, 'No. As a matter of fact, Lance isn't her father anyway. My first husband was killed soon after she was born.'

'Forgive me. I didn't know.' But the information interested him; I could see that. 'They seem very fond of each other,' he added after a moment. 'That must be a great comfort to you.'

I opened my mouth to give the usual, meaningless affirmative, but he turned his head and the force of those black eyes dried up the lie stillborn. He said very softly, 'I have the impression that you're deeply concerned about your daughter.'

To my horror I felt tears rush into my eyes. Immediately his hand, warm and surprisingly large, closed over mine on the railing. 'I must apologise—I'd no right whatever—Please put it down to an almost instinctive desire to be of

50

help. No doubt you'd like me to leave you.'

I shook my head helplessly and held on to the comforting hand, while the grass, the flowers and the group of girls gradually cleared before my blurred gaze. He said gently, 'I have intruded unpardonably, but if you ever need me, my Bury number is in the directory.' He smiled a little. 'I'm afraid I don't carry cards in my swimming trunks!'

I nodded, still incapable of speech, and after a moment to allow me to collect myself, he moved away. Beside me Cynthia's voice said lightly, 'What an odd little man! Darling, don't you positively *hate* all that fur? Men seem to be so proud of it, but give me a smooth bronzed torso like your gorgeous Lance's any day! Frankly your new friend reminds me of something out of *Planet of the Apes!*'

I laughed a little shakily, grateful to her for restoring my precarious control. 'Actually he's rather sweet. I wouldn't be surprised if he's foreign. There's an odd inflection in his voice sometimes, though of course he speaks perfect English.'

'*Chacqu'un à son goût!*' She gave a little shiver and glanced up at a bank of clouds which was forming to the east. 'It looks as though we've had the best of the day. I hope it's not going to rain.'

The buffet was finished, the long table a litter of dirty plates haphazardly stacked. Mark and the Pomfrett children, who had already

51

returned to the pool area, were now coming back again, pulling on sweaters and cardigans.

'There's quite a breeze getting up,' Roger remarked. 'We've decided to move inside and suffer the Sunday film, if that's okay?'

'As long as you go in the study,' Lance replied. The six young people came up the steps and moved in a body through the french windows. Briony and Mark were hand in hand and I saw Lance's lips tighten as they passed.

The rest of us, determined to stay outdoors, returned to the edge of the pool, but the breeze Roger had mentioned was distinctly cool, whipping along the surface of the water, and the clouds had increased and darkened threateningly. For about half an hour we sat huddled in sweaters then, ominously, a large fat raindrop splattered on to the concrete beside me. As though it were a signal, we all scrambled to our feet, gathering belongings together as the first slow drops fell with separate little plops into the pool. The young people had of course left a litter of dark glasses, wet costumes and suntan oil behind them, and I gathered these into one armful to be sorted out later. By the time we reached the house the raindrops had merged to become a steady downpour, drilling relentlessly on the terrace and beating a rustling tattoo on the laden trees. We followed one another hastily through the french windows, laughing and exclaiming and shaking the rain off our hair: and above the confused mêlée Max Forrest's compelling voice reached us clearly:

'What an absolutely extraordinary painting!'

Immediately there was silence, while everyone registered that this was the first time he had seen it. He was standing in front of it with his hands behind his back, gazing up at it in total absorption. Simon, with a wink at the rest of us, said laughingly, 'How about an analysis of it, Max? What do you read into it?'

Lance, who had just come through the french windows, stopped dead, instantly summing up the position. 'I think a cup of tea would warm everyone,' he began, but Stella gestured to him to be quiet.

'We're just asking Max to analyse your painting.'

'*Your* painting?' Max turned sharply. Across the room he and Lance stared at each other.

'Well, now that Stella's given the game away,' Simon said disgustedly, 'we might as well admit—'

'But you didn't paint it.' The statement cut flatly across Simon's voice.

Edgar said indignantly, 'He most certainly did! Surely you must have seen it before? It's very well known—made Lance's fortune for him years ago.'

Max ignored him. His eyes hadn't left Lance. 'Are you telling me that you painted that picture?'

53

Paula gave a light embarrassed laugh. 'Darling, even if he isn't, everyone else is! Don't make such a meal of it!'

Max relaxed slightly. 'I beg your pardon. I was so—'

'Well, come on!' Simon insisted. 'What do you think of it? You're a head-shrinker—give us your opinion. What is it trying to say?'

Max smiled a little. 'Head-shrinker I might be, art critic I definitely am not. However, that painting undoubtedly has a certain quality which—reaches out for you.'

Almost against my will, my eyes were drawn back to the hated canvas. In the premature gloom it glowed with a weird unearthly beauty. Max went on slowly, addressing Lance now, who still stood motionless just inside the room.

'I must apologise for my outspokenness. I admit to considerable surprise to learn you're the artist of this painting.'

'But why?' Stella asked curiously, for all of us.

'It's hard to say. After all, Lance and I hardly know each other. I realise that. But— well, he seems to have developed very differently from what I'd have expected on the basis of this picture. However, you say it was done some time ago.' His voice tailed off and for all his politeness I could see he was still not convinced. Everyone waited and after a moment he went on: 'There's a basic insecurity about it—a longing for changelessness but an acknowledgement, in those worn and weary faces, that such things cannot be. Eternal youth—' he leant forward to read the title on the frame—'or spring, or whatever is granted to very few and they pay a high price for it.'

'A high price?' Cynthia echoed a little nervously.

'Of course. They die young.'

My eyes flew from the dark, intelligent face to Lance's white one. He had put out a hand to the wall as though to steady himself and instinctively I moved over to him and took his arm. He didn't seem to notice me. His face had a shuttered, in-turned look which frightened me.

Edgar cleared his throat uncomfortably and Simon said with a forced laugh, 'Well, that's quite an eye-opener! Not thinking of charging a consultation fee are you, Max?'

Max smiled deprecatingly and turned at last from the painting. For a long moment his eyes again held Lance's and I felt the tremor that went through him like a high voltage shock-wave. Yet even as I battled with conflicting emotions of anxiety for Lance and indignation against Max, I knew in my heart that the little doctor had unerringly pinpointed the essence of what had made me hate and fear the painting so much. It had an undeniable aura of approaching death.

I said in a rush, 'Darling you're cold and this sweater's quite wet. You'd better go and change. You mentioned tea—I think we could all do with some. Light the gas fire, Stella, if you're cold. I'll go and ask Mrs Rose to put the kettle on.'

By the time I returned to the room the tension had evaporated and they were sitting chatting in little groups, the men particularly looking strangely incongruous with their bare legs in the rather formal atmosphere of the room. Someone had closed the windows and the rain continued to beat heavily against the glass. Lance, still pale beneath his tan, was talking more or less normally to Edgar and Cynthia.

Simon pulled out the coffee table for me and I lowered the tray on to it. Behind me the door opened again and Briony's voice, oddly taut, said a little too brightly, 'I thought I heard the rattle of cups! Anything to eat?'

'Good heavens, child!' Cynthia exclaimed. 'It's hardly any time since lunch! What it must be to have a ravening appetite and still remain slender and sylph-like. Youth, blessed youth!'

'I gather the film's over?' Lance commented.

'Yes, thank goodness.'

'Wasn't it much good?'

'It was horrible!' declared Rachel Forrest—or was it Rebecca?—perching on the arm of her mother's chair. 'All about reincarnation and spirits and things.'

In the distance a low growl of thunder underlined her words.

56

'Put the lights on, Briony,' I said sharply, 'I can hardly see what I'm doing. Half the tea will be in the saucers. And there's a plate of biscuits here if you're convinced you can't last till supper.'

'Reincarnation?' Paula repeated with lifted eyebrows. 'Hardly in the classification of light entertainment, surely?'

'It's a load of rubbish,' Simon said flatly.

'Nevertheless,' Roger put in, 'about two-thirds of the world's population believe in it. Actually, I find the whole idea fascinating. And you know, biologically it makes pretty good sense. Just imagine if everyone and everything which has ever lived goes on living after death. Boy, the population explosion we keep hearing about would have nothing on the problems they'd have to cope with in the spirit world!'

'You mean all of us sitting here now might have been alive before?' his sister Lindsay asked, round-eyed.

'Probably, yes. It's against the law of nature, after all, for energy to be wasted. Mind you, I'm not saying I definitely believe in it, only that it's an intriguing concept. And incidentally it was one of the Christian dogmas, too, before they came up with original sin.'

Simon said suspiciously, 'You seem to know a lot about it. When did you start taking an interest in this kind of thing?'

'There's a book in the school library on

57

comparative religions. It certainly makes you stop and think.'

I handed the last cup and saucer to Lance, noticing with concern how much his hand was shaking. From him I automatically glanced at Briony and felt a further stirring of unease. She was sitting rigidly on the sofa holding tightly to Mark's hand and her eyes were wide and frightened. I didn't understand what was upsetting her but I cast about frantically for a natural means of changing the conversation. Before I could think of anything, Rebecca said encouragingly, 'Go on then, Roger. How does it work? Can you choose when you'll be born again?'

Roger glanced apologetically at his parents. 'Views vary on that. Some people say yes, which is why, even when there's no medical reason, some women can't have babies. A soul apparently doesn't choose to have them as parents.'

'Thanks very much,' said Cynthia, drily. 'And before you all start looking askance at me, let me make it quite clear that no soul was ever given the chance of choosing me! Edgar and I opted out of the procreation stakes quite voluntarily and believe me we've never regretted it!' Her tone implied that she was regretting it less than ever at the present moment.

Roger, who had flushed during this interruption, repeated hastily, 'As I said, that's

58

only one theory. One of the main beliefs is that how you behave in this existence conditions you for the next, and so on.'

'I think that's quite enough from you,' put in his father firmly. 'Over to you, Max. Shoot him down in flames!'

Max bent forward to replace his cup and saucer on the table. 'I don't want to bore you all with a psychological dissertation, but obviously in our line of business we feel that all such theories are indicative of the state of mind of those holding them. It's the mind itself, though not many people appreciate it, which is one of the greatest mysteries of the universe.'

Outside the windows the garden was now obscured by a curtain of heavy rain and it was almost as dark as night. The thunder had moved closer and Max had to wait for its roll to finish before continuing.

'The power of the mind can be devastating. Most of the so-called supernatural occurrences can be put down to some form of telepathy or mind control.'

'From what Roger said about a soul taking over a body,' interrupted one of his daughters—they'd changed places since I last pinpointed them and I was no longer sure which was which—'it sounds rather like possession, and I shouldn't fancy that.'

'You need not worry!' her father replied. 'Possession is much more likely to be by one's own neuroses than by any outside force.'

'But there *are* genuine cases of possession,' Roger insisted. 'Look at exorcism and all the rest of it.'

'I confess,' said Max smoothly, 'that there is a great deal we still don't understand. Nevertheless, I repeat that most disturbances of that nature originate in the mind—perhaps by means of dual or even multiple personality.'

As he finished speaking there was a deafening peal of thunder directly overhead and all the lights went out. One of the girls gave a little scream and even I, in my own sitting-room, experienced a moment of sheer primitive terror. Then Edgar flicked his lighter and in its wavery light we all looked at one another and laughed shame-facedly.

'Stage effects and all!' Simon commented. 'A fuse seems to have blown. Got any fuse wire, Lance?'

I stood up. 'It's no use asking him—he wouldn't know what to do with it if he had! I'll go and see if I can find out what's happened.'

'Perhaps I can help,' Edgar volunteered. I hesitated, but as it would have seemed odd to argue, I made my way out of the room, Edgar close behind me.

From the far end of the hall came Mrs Rose's hesitant voice. 'Are all the lights out, ma'am?'

'All the downstairs ones, anyway. We're just going to see what we can do. In the meantime, Mrs Rose, would you take a few candles into the sitting-room if you can lay your hands on them. I seem to remember we bought a stock during the last power cuts. The fuse box is in the cloakroom,' I added over my shoulder to Edgar.

The stairs loomed on our right and I swerved to avoid them. Only a very faint light was coming through the glass of the front door, more a diffused darkness. The cloakroom lay directly ahead and I moved cautiously inside. I realised I was trembling and was not sure whether it was from cold—the temperature must have dropped ten degrees in the last hour—or from the awareness of Edgar close behind me. Two days ago I wouldn't have given his presence a second thought. He still had his lighter flaring and was bending beside me over the fuse box. I thought wildly—I can't just go off and leave him! It would look so stupid! And then, blessedly, a flickering light blossomed in the doorway as Mrs Rose appeared with her candles.

'Here you are, sir, this should help.'

'Oh thank you.' I took one gratefully and held it up for Edgar. He was fiddling with the card of fuse wire and I watched him in silence. After a moment he sat back and simultaneously there was a concerted cheer from the direction of the sitting-room and the light from its open door spilled into the hall. Edgar stood up slowly and, steadying my hand with his, blew out the candle I held.

'You're cold,' he said quietly.

'Yes. Thanks so much. Lance is absolutely useless round the house! I've become quite adept now at changing plugs and things.' I hurried out into the hall before he could reply and reached the sitting-room to find the others coming out.

'You're not going already?' It was seldom before seven that we had the house to ourselves on a Sunday evening.

'The girls are shivering,' Paula said apologetically. 'I think we should go home and change into something more suitable. Don't worry about an umbrella'—I had turned to the stand—'we're dressed for water anyway!'

The worst of the storm had passed and it was already getting lighter again. Within minutes everyone had gone. As the last of them drove away I closed the door and turned to Lance and Briony. Both of them looked pale and strained. Distractedly I tried to think back. They had both been all right at lunch. I could pin Lance's discomfort to all the talk about the painting, a familiar enough cause of stress in this family, but all I could think of in Briony's case was that perhaps she and Mark had quarrelled. Yet she'd been holding on to his hand just before the lights went out, when Roger was talking about that ridiculous film. Could it have been that which had upset her? I wondered as we moved back into the deserted sitting-room.

Trying to restore a more normal atmosphere, I remarked, 'They're a strange family, the Forrests. I'm not sure they fitted in all that well.'

'No,' Lance replied abruptly. 'Frankly, I rather regretted inviting them. I can't say I cared for the man over much. Rather an inflated opinion of himself, I thought. His wife and family seemed pleasant enough, though.'

Briony had moved automatically over to the painting and Lance's eyes followed her compulsively, full of a strange yearning. After a moment she laid her arms along the mantelshelf and rested her head on them.

'What is it, darling? Another headache?'

'I think one's coming on, yes.' Her voice was muffled. 'It's probably the thunder.' She turned, her face drawn. 'I think if you don't mind I'll go upstairs. If the headache clears I've some revision I ought to do, and if it doesn't— well, darkness and rest are the only things that help.'

'I ought to do some more work too,' Lance said, still in that clipped voice, as she went out of the room. 'We fixed Stella's first sitting for Tuesday morning and I'm at college all day tomorrow. I'd like to finish off the canvas I'm working on.'

'Not now, surely?' I protested.

'It's as good a time as any. We've a good two hours in hand, since they've all gone so early.' He glanced at my face and added more gently,

63

'You look in need of a rest. Why don't you settle down with the Sunday papers until supper time?'

And before I could reply he had pushed open the french windows and gone out into the rain.

CHAPTER FOUR

Throughout the following day, I was haunted by the feeling that we were all marking time, that some traumatic climax was rushing towards us and until it actually reached and engulfed us there was nothing we could do to protect ourselves.

At breakfast we all showed signs of strain. Briony, pale and listless, shaded her eyes from the uncaring brightness of the sun.

'Another headache?' I asked anxiously.

'The same one, actually. It lasted all night.'

'Have you taken your migraine pills?'

'Yes, but they never work.'

'I think you should go back to bed, dear.'

'Oh Mother, I can't! There's far too much going on at the moment. I can't afford to miss anything, with the exams only a month away.'

'But you're in no state to take anything in anyway.' Suppose she had one of those strange spells at school? She might already have had one. At the back of my mind an echo of Max's voice was murmuring something which I couldn't recall but which I felt might be important.

'Don't fuss, Mother,' Briony said gently.

'If you insist on going, at least promise you'll phone if you feel really ill. I could be there in ten minutes.'

'I promise. Any chance of a lift, Daddy?'

'Only one way, I'm afraid. My last lecture finishes at three-thirty today so you'll have to make your own way home.'

'That's all right, I'm meeting Mark anyway.'

Lance folded his napkin with deliberate restraint. 'Don't you think,' he began quietly, 'that you're seeing rather too much of young Mark? Friday, Saturday, Sunday, and now today too?'

'Oh don't be stuffy, darling! I need a bit of relaxation and so does he. If you'll hang on I'll just get my school bag and then I'm ready.' The door swung to behind her.

He looked across at me challengingly. 'Now don't start telling me I'm being possessive again. Don't *you* think she's seeing too much of him?'

'Not really. After all, she keeps to the rule of no mid-week dates during term time. He'll only be walking back from school with her.'

'It's this implication that they can't let a day pass without seeing each other which I find rather hard to take.'

'Weren't you the same at her age?'

'At her age, or very little older, I was doing

65

my National Service.'

'But not in a monastery, I presume?'

He smiled slightly. 'All right, I'm being unreasonable. You're probably right.'

'Okay, chauffeur!' She had appeared in the doorway again, still pale but smiling determinedly. Lance stood up, patting his pocket to check that he had his keys.

'By the way, Ann, will you ask Moira to be sure to write to that new framing firm which sent us its price list? It sounded quite reasonable. And there's the letter from the Arts Council that came on Saturday. I've left it on her desk.'

'I'll have a word with her.'

The front door closed behind them and another long day stretched ahead of me. Moira Cassidy was Lance's part-time secretary who came three days a week to look after the business side of his work—arranging loans to galleries, exhibitions and so on and keeping notes in the large desk diary of his various engagements. Two of her days coincided with Lance's days at college. He had found that if he was available she kept distracting him with queries which she could really deal with quite adequately herself. He therefore left her taped messages and they held a weekly conference on Friday mornings. It seemed to work well. It was ridiculous to resent Moira, but I knew that I did. I would have been only too happy to have taken over her work for Lance, but my tentative offer, early in our marriage, had been brushed aside. 'Nonsense, of course I couldn't let you work for me. Anyway, Moira has all the contacts.'

In the same way, there were times when I resented Mrs Rose—'Rosie' to both Lance and Briony, though I'd never managed to achieve such informality myself—who made me feel in the way in my own kitchen, as the Giffords, father and son, resented any attempts I might make at gardening. I was expected to supervise, instruct, admire—and sit in a deck chair. 'My shrubs' and 'my annuals', it was tacitly implied, were to be left strictly to those who knew how to deal with them.

Slowly I stood up and pushed my chair back under the table. There wasn't even any need to clear the dishes. I paused for a moment to glance through the open door of the little office, sandwiched at the back of the hall between kitchen and cloak room. The sunshine had already reached one corner of it, falling across the desk and the dark mound of the covered typewriter. On the black surface lay a sheet of paper, doubtless the letter to which Lance had referred.

Half my resentment of Moira was caused by the conviction that she despised me for what must have seemed my uselessness. I couldn't blame her. She herself was divorced and lived in a small flat in Rushyford with her widowed mother. She would have tidied the flat and prepared the old lady's lunch before arriving here at the Lodge on the dot of nine o'clock to deal efficiently with Lance's correspondence. And on the days that he didn't require her, she worked on the cash desk of one of the local supermarkets.

Even as I stood there broodingly there was the sound of a car drawing up outside, a light step on the gravel, and Moira's voice behind me. 'Good morning, Mrs Tenby. Another lovely day after the storm.'

I roused myself, 'Yes, indeed. By the way, my husband asked me to remind you about the framers—'

'That's all right. I wrote to them on Friday.' She briskly removed her gloves and placed them with her neat, square handbag on top of the filing cabinet. 'And I presume that's the letter about the travelling exhibition? It'll be rather tight getting the Council the pictures they want. The exhibition starts the week after the Lavenham showing. Still, no doubt Bourlets will cope as usual.'

As she spoke she was neatly slitting open the morning post which Mrs Rose had left on her desk, her long fingers quick and methodical. Everything about her carried through the impression of efficiency: her fair hair tidily pinned up into a no-nonsense pleat, large eyes behind large horn-rimmed spectacles, large mouth, large straight teeth for which she'd doubtless needed a brace as a child. 'All the

68

better to eat you with!' I thought facetiously. She was the personification of the perfect secretary, even to staying uncomplainingly overnight on the few occasions when pressure of work demanded it, and sleeping perfectly contentedly in the attic bedroom across the landing from Mrs Rose. At such times I had at first attempted to inveigle her into one of the guest rooms, invited her to eat with us, and so on, but my tentative overtures had been firmly and politely declined. In Moira Cassidy's eyes she was one of the staff, and she had no intention of mixing socially with us. In the same way she would never attend any of our open days or parties unless specifically requested by Lance and then strictly for business reasons.

'Can I do anything for you, Mrs Tenby?'

Translation, I thought ironically: Please stop hovering and let those of us who have work to do get on with it in peace!

'No, thank you.' Obediently I closed the door and a moment later the quick staccato tapping of the typewriter reached my ears. Lance would have dropped Briony at school by now. Anxiously I hoped she would be all right.

Across the hall the telephone shrilled, making me jump. The tapping behind the closed door stopped as Moira waited to see if I would take the call. It was probably for Lance anyway, but I picked up the phone and was unusually glad to hear Cynthia's voice

69

over the wire.

'Ann darling, you are free this afternoon, aren't you? I was speaking to Paula Forrest at your place yesterday, and guess what? She plays bridge! Isn't that a stroke of luck? I think I can probably coax Stella to make up a four—if she's not ensconced with Lance, that is.'

'The sittings don't start until tomorrow.' I hesitated. Bridge would be one way of passing the afternoon, but I felt it might be diplomatic not to become too friendly with Paula Forrest. I knew Lance would not invite them again and if we were seeing a lot of each other this could be embarrassing.

'Well?' Cynthia demanded impatiently. 'Are you free or aren't you?'

'Yes. Thanks, Cynthia, I'd love to come.'

'Fine. My place at two, then.'

I replaced the receiver. In the office the machine had already started up again. I smiled a little grimly to myself. Bridge in the afternoon—the height of middle-class decadence! It was just as well I'd answered the phone myself.

The morning dragged on. I had coffee. I watered the house plants. I changed the flowers in the sitting-room bowl. And wherever I went I seemed to be followed by the ticking of clocks. I hadn't realised we had so many in the house. Tick, tock. Tick, tock. Slowly, with inexorable deliberation, time was passing,

70

bringing us nearer to—what?

I was thankful when it was time to drive the short distance up the road to Cynthia and Edgar's house.

'My goodness,' Stella remarked as she swiftly dealt the cards, 'Lance is a forceful character, isn't he? I happened to mention that Tuesday is my day for the hairdresser and he just said, 'Cancel it!' My dear, he can't have any idea of how ghastly I look if I miss that weekly ritual!'

I laughed. 'But you must admit that an earth mother is unlikely to sport a perm!'

'*Earth mother?* Ye gods, is that how he sees me? And there was I thinking I'd be all Gainsborough-like and glamorous! Does that mean I can't have my hair done till the thing's finished? It could take weeks!'

'He won't be concentrating on your hair for weeks,' I said consolingly.

'You should wear it short as I do,' Paula remarked, 'then you could wash it yourself.'

Paula's hair was certainly short, but cut in a severe style which most people would find hard to wear. It was part of her twenties image no doubt, as was the shapeless—but pure silk—dress which hung on her rather bony body. To complete the picture a lorgnette was attached to the long beads round her neck. Paula was in fact very short-sighted but she had turned the defect to maximum advantage. Very sophisticated, I thought, and rather unapproachable. I wondered if Max had ever tried to analyse his wife, and my thought was echoed in part by Cynthia, who, having played a hand, said interestedly:

'Do tell us all about that brilliant husband of yours, Paula. I hardly dared open my mouth in his presence for fear of incriminating myself!'

'I don't suppose he considers people he meets socially in that way,' Stella put in comfortably.

'Actually I'm not so sure.' Casually Paula played a trump and scooped up the hand. 'It's so much a part of his life that he can't help mentally assessing people, whether he means to or not.' Unwillingly I remembered Max's attentive examination of the painting and the blind, closed look on Lance's face, and tried without success to dispel the lingering sense of unease latent in the memory.

'But is there much call for work of that kind here?' Stella was asking. 'I should have thought the English were too phlegmatic and down to earth to need psychiatrists. Surely he'd do better in America or somewhere, where everybody seems to have one!'

Paula smiled slightly. 'I'm sure that Max's reply to that would be that it's the seemingly phlegmatic who often turn out to be a positive mass of repression and buried neuroses. But seriously, a lot more attention is being paid to mental health, even here, than there ever used to be.'

'Not in Rushyford, surely?' objected Cynthia, raising her finely pencilled eyebrows. 'His consulting rooms are in Bury but he has days at various psychiatric wards round about.'

'It must be fascinating,' Cynthia remarked with an envious sigh. 'Really, you know, I do find it rather galling. Your husbands are all so *interesting*! Max is all clued up on psychology, Lance is a brilliant artist, and Simon is so devastatingly handsome that it raises one's morale just to be seen with him. And what have I managed to achieve? Edgar!'

It was impossible not to laugh, but I felt a niggling sense of disloyalty. Edgar might not be brilliant or an oil painting but he was kind and steady and dependable, attributes which didn't necessarily apply to the other three.

The afternoon wore on. My mind was only half on the game, but we weren't playing too seriously and it didn't seem to matter. I had the impression that Paula had expected a higher standard and I did not doubt that the next time Cynthia hopefully rang for a bridge date, Mrs Forrest would regretfully have a prior engagement. It struck me as amusing that I should have worried about becoming too friendly with Paula. Obviously she chose her own friends, and there would not be many who received her confidences.

The last rubber, as was often the case, took a long time to finish, and it was almost six o'clock when I finally returned to Fairfield Lodge. It was on occasions like this that I guiltily showered blessings on Mrs Rose, who would have the dinner preparations well in hand. With an increased spurt of anxiety about Briony I hurried into the house.

I knew immediately that something was wrong and I turned without hesitation into the sitting-room. Briony was lying in a crumpled little heap on the hearth-rug.

For a moment time stopped completely. Then, without consciously moving, I was kneeling beside her, gently turning her head aside. Her face had been buried in the soft deep pile and I honestly think I was surprised to find her still breathing. Scrambling to my feet, I pulled and tugged frantically at the window catches, staggered on to the terrace and, gripping the stone balustrade until it bit into my fingers, I called Lance.

Urgency must have permeated my voice, because he appeared round the bank of shrubbery almost at once. 'What is it? What's the matter?'

'Briony's fainted. Hurry!' And I turned and stumbled back inside. He was with me almost by the time I reached her again. He said rapidly under his breath, 'Oh God, God, God!'

'She's still breathing,' I said foolishly.

'So I see.' Gently he scooped his arms underneath her and carried her to the sofa. 'You telephone the doctor—tell him it's an

74

emergency. I'll stay with her.'

I didn't question his instructions. He was always the one Briony wanted when she was ill. Even as a baby waking in the night, it had been for him that she cried.

I returned from the phone to find him kneeling beside her chafing her limp hand. Her breathing was rapid and shallow and there was still no sign of returning consciousness.

'She should never have gone to school today,' Lance said accusingly.

'I tried to stop her. You heard me.'

'I should have waited and brought her home with me.'

Briony stirred slightly and gave a little moaning sigh. Her eyes flickered for a moment, then opened and stared blankly up at Lance's face. He lifted her hand and brushed it with his lips. 'It's all right, darling—all over now.'

'What happened?'

'I don't know. We found you on the floor. You probably fainted.'

There was a puzzled look on her face that I didn't care for. I moved forward and smoothed the hair back from her forehead. 'Is your head still bad, darling?'

'No, no I'm fine. I just need to rest a wee while, that's all.' She closed her eyes and turned her head away slightly. Rest a wee while? What a curious—I suddenly became heart-stoopingly aware of Lance's rigidity. He was still kneeling, staring down at the girl as though he could X-ray her mind with his naked eyes. For a moment I was convinced he was going to pass out as well. I gripped hold of his shoulders.

'Darling, what is it? Are you all right?'

There was no response and I shook him frantically. His glazed eyes came up to my face without recognition. 'Lance! Help me to get her upstairs before the doctor comes. Can you stand?' I held his arm and he stumblingly got to his feet, swaying slightly. 'Had you better sit down for a moment? It's been a shock—'

'A shock,' he repeated expressionlessly. And laughed. Somehow the sound was itself shocking. Visibly he braced himself and after a moment lifted Briony off the sofa. 'I'm all right. I can manage her.'

She gave a little sigh and nestled her head under his chin. I saw his teeth fasten involuntarily in his lip.

In the hall we came to face with Mrs Rose. 'Is something wrong, sir? I heard Mrs Tenby call.' Her voice trailed away as her widening eyes fastened on Briony.

'She fainted,' Lance said briefly, making for the stairs. 'It's all right, we've phoned for the doctor.' He kicked open her bedroom door before I could reach it and laid her down on the bed. Then he turned and faced me. 'It's after six. Where have you been?'

'At Cynthia's, playing bridge.' Ridiculous to feel so guilty. I added gently, 'Relax, darling,

76

she's breathing normally now. The doctor will tell us what to do.'

But Dr Burton was not much help. 'As I said before, Mrs Tenby, there doesn't seem any serious cause for these attacks. Girls of her age often have fainting spells, you know. Fortunately the rug cushioned her fall, so we haven't the added complication of concussion. Was she out in the sun at the weekend? In this country people never treat it with the respect it deserves. 'Mad dogs and Englishmen,' you know, but in large doses it can be lethal, even here.'

Lance stayed up in the bedroom with Briony and on the way downstairs I said softly, 'I've just learnt that she seems to have bouts of amnesia as well, doctor. I'm really rather worried about it.'

He frowned. 'What happened exactly?'

Stumblingly, keeping an ear open for Lance, I repeated what Jan had told me on Friday afternoon.

'That does put rather a different complexion on things,' he admitted as I came to the end. 'It might be an idea for her to see a psychiatrist.'

I stared at him fearfully. 'You think there's something seriously wrong after all?'

'No, Mrs Tenby,' he repeated patiently. 'I don't think anything of the sort. We've already ascertained that there's no tumour or any abnormal pressure. I'm merely concerned with getting to the root of what's bothering her, and

77

for that a qualified psychiatrist has more means at his disposal than I have. If you like I could give you a letter—'

'Do you know Dr Forrest?' I interrupted.

'Yes indeed, a very able man. Would you like him to see her?'

'I'm—not sure, Doctor. May I think about it first?'

'Of course. Naturally you'll want to discuss it with your husband. Let me know what you decide. In the meantime, see she has plenty of rest and I'd like to see her again in a couple of days.'

'Very well. Thank you.'

I stood at the open door until his car had disappeared in the stream of homeward-bound traffic. My heart was thumping against my ribs and I felt slightly sick. Contrary to the doctor's assumption, my procrastination was not to enable me to discuss the matter with Lance, but merely to give me time to accept the inevitability of the decision. For I knew that if I did decide to take Briony to Max professionally, it would be without Lance's knowledge or consent.

CHAPTER FIVE

That night was another sleepless one for me. My brain refused to stop its tortuous weaving round and round the events of the last few days, and in particular kept reminding me of my swift, instinctive prayer that evening, that it would be as herself that Briony regained consciousness. Worst of all, I wasn't entirely sure that the prayer had been granted. The more I repeated to myself those first few words she had spoken, the more frightened I became. There had been something alien there, an intonation, a choice of words which surely were not Briony's. That Lance had noticed it too I had no doubt.

For the first time I was forced to face the fact that since to our knowledge she had never actually lost consciousness before, those other times when she had 'gone away', someone else must have been standing in for her. And right on cue my brain supplied the remark of Max's which had been tantalising my memory at breakfast. 'Most disturbances of that kind originate in the mind, perhaps by means of dual or even multiple personality.' The peal of thunder and subsequent fusing of the lights had put an end to the conversation, but what had he meant? What in the name of heaven was dual personality? And Jan's voice answered patly in my head, 'Mark calls it "going away".'

My eyes flew open, staring sightlessly at the dark ceiling. Could the two things really be interconnected? Was it remotely possible? Surely dual personality was just a fanciful way of describing schizophrenia? The word crawled

79

over my mind like some hideous spider and I recoiled violently. Only one thing seemed clear to me, and that was that I had to see Max as soon as possible. I couldn't confide my fears to Lance, since I was far from happy about his own attitude. Like a mouse down a new tunnel, my mind scuttled back to the frozen horror with which he had reacted to Briony's waking words that evening.

Lance and Briony—Lance and Briony. I was convinced that both of them were threatened in some subtle and horrible way and that I was powerless to help them. Tossing and turning, alternately throwing off the bedclothes and pulling them back again, I spent one of the most tormented nights of my life.

I had intended to let Briony sleep as long as possible the next morning and was completely taken aback when she appeared at the breakfast table dressed for school.

'Darling, you can't possibly go today! If you'd only stayed home yesterday as I suggested, we might have avoided all the trouble last night.'

'I'm quite all right now—really.' She calmly sat down at the table and poured some cereal into a bowl. She looked up and smiled as she caught my worried gaze. 'Honestly, Mother, I promise I am. Not even a headache. I've slept it all off.'

'But the doctor said you were to rest. I don't know what he—'

'I *have* rested, continuously, for about thirteen hours. I'm fine now and I must go today because we're having a French test. I can't afford to miss it.'

'Lance, you speak to her!' I demanded helplessly. He was staring at her with a yearning intentness which sent a prickle up my back.

'You're quite sure you feel all right now?' he asked at last.

'Yes, Daddy, really. Don't worry.'

'Don't worry!' I repeated. 'I come home and find you out cold on the floor and you tell me not to worry!'

'But that was yesterday,' she replied patiently. '*Please* don't fuss, darlings. I know you're thinking of what's best for me, but you know I have got a bit of sense and if I really didn't feel up to going today I wouldn't. And I promise to ring if I do feel ill.'

'I'll run you down anyway,' Lance said, preparing to stand up.

'No, there's no need. It's not one of your college days and the fresh air will blow the last of the cobwebs away.' She finished her orange juice and rose from the table. 'I hope you get off to a good start with Mrs Pomfret.'

'Oh hell!' Lance said under his breath. 'Is it today she's coming?'

I watched Briony leave the room with a sinking of my heart. 'I really don't think she should go.'

'Short of locking her in her room, there doesn't seem to be any way to stop her. Is there any chance of putting Stella off, do you think?' I smiled, trying to dismiss my uneasiness. 'Not now she's cancelled her hair appointment! Have you decided how you want to portray her?'

'Vaguely. I brought a few clothes back from the modelling box at college. Peasanty things—blouse, apron, full skirt—you know the kind of thing.' He rubbed a hand across his eyes. 'I couldn't feel less like starting a new picture. In fact, I don't feel like working at all.'

'Well, you never do much at the first sitting, do you? It's just a question of getting to know the person behind the face.'

'But I already know Stella. And anyway this isn't a portrait in the strict sense. I visualise the composition as a field—corn growing or something—and the figure of this country girl sitting gazing out across it.' He flashed me a brief smile. 'It worked, didn't it? You managed to reawaken my interest. Thanks. All right, I'll suffer Stella as arranged and if the worst comes to the worst, doodle the hour away.' He paused and suddenly reached out to pat my hand. 'Try not to worry about Briony. She'll be all right.'

I sat staring after him, my eyes stinging with tears. The brief, instinctive gesture touched me, even if there was no more in it than a passing desire to comfort.

The morning wore on. Stella duly arrived

82

and made her way round to the studio. An hour later she reappeared, tapping at the french window of the sitting-room. I went to let her in. 'How did it go?'

'Search me! We sat in silence most of the time. I'm stiff as a board from trying to keep still. Any chance of a coffee?'

'Yes, it should be here any minute. I asked Mrs Rose to put a cup out for you.'

'You know, for all the work the blasted man did today, I could have had my hair done after all!'

'Poor Stella, that really is a deprivation isn't it? When's your next sitting?'

'Friday at the same time. Ah, coffee! Salvation!'

When Stella had gone I strolled across the garden to the studio. Lance was leaning back in his chair staring out of the window. The canvas in front of him contained a few charcoal lines which uncannily suggested Stella's profile.

'Still not in the mood?'

'Afraid not. Was she bored stiff? I couldn't even rouse myself to talk to her.'

'You told me not to worry about Briony,' I reminded him quietly.

He didn't meet my eyes. 'I must admit I'm not very happy about her blacking out like that. There's no way of knowing how long she'd been lying there. If she went in straight after school it could have been over an hour.'

'Dr Burton says a lot of girls her age have

fainting fits. He's seeing her again tomorrow, to check that everything's all right.' And if it wasn't, I thought, I would have no choice but to see Max. The night's urgency had mitigated slightly and once more I was aware of putting off contacting him. 'Are you coming back for lunch or staying here?'

'Oh, I'll come. There's no muse to interrupt today.' He stood up and stretched. 'What are you doing this afternoon?'

'Nothing special. I don't seem able to settle to anything today.'

He smiled, putting a careless arm across my shoulders. 'Poor little mother hen!'

'You know you're just as worried yourself.'

'Is there any point in ringing the school to make sure she's all right?'

'She'd never forgive us. Anyway, she promised to phone if she wasn't. Work might be the best thing for her—take her mind off it.'

After lunch I sat out in the deck chair again and rather to my surprise fell asleep in the warm sun. I only awoke properly when Mrs Rose brought out the tea tray at four-thirty.

'Goodness, is it that time already? Is Miss Briony home?'

'Not yet, ma'am, but I thought I'd better not hold back your tea any longer.'

'She'll probably be here any minute.' I poured a cup for Lance and carried it across the grass. He was staring out of the window again, with no indication of having done any

work at all. He turned sharply at my approach.
'Well, how is she?'
'She's not back yet. The test has probably
delayed them. Here's your tea, anyway.'
He said restlessly, 'I wish she'd come. I can't
help feeling rather anxious.'
'Me too. Since you're not working, I'll bring
my cup and join you.'
Minutes later I lowered myself gingerly on to
the stool where Stella had sat that morning. I
glanced at my watch for the second time in two
minutes, and resolved not to look at it again
until Briony was walking over the grass
towards us. She was sure to be home before
we'd finished tea. Yet slowly as I drank it, there
was still no sign of her. The restlessness
returned.
'I think I'll go and have a bath. I'm all sticky
from sleeping in the sun.'
'It's really rather inconsiderate of her,'
Lance said edgily. 'She should have realised
we'd be a bit anxious today.'
'She's probably chatting with her friends,
comparing answers.'
'All the same—'
'She won't be long now.'
Although I had needed his company, his
concern was now almost outweighing mine
and I couldn't withstand them both. I put the
deck chair away in the shed, playing a futile
game with myself. She'll be home before I
reach the terrace—by the time I've put the

chair away—before I go inside. But the shed door was shut and padlocked, the tea tray returned to Mrs Rose, and still there was no sign of Briony.

If she's not back by the time I've had my bath, I'll start phoning her friends, I told myself, and there was a little comfort at the thought of positive action. It was nonsense to worry because a seventeen-year-old girl was—what?—forty minutes late home from school, and in broad daylight too. But Briony hadn't looked well that morning, despite the brave act she had put on, and she was usually very punctilious about phoning to let us know if she was going to be late.

I kept the bathroom door open while I ran the water so that I could hear the front door, bathed quickly and had just stepped out of the water when the telephone shrilled through the house. I dragged a towel round my dripping body and ran barefoot to the bedroom.

'Hello? Briony?'

There was a brief pause and then a boy's voice answered, 'No, it's Mark, Mrs Tenby. I was phoning to find out how Briony is.'

'You didn't meet her after school, then?'

'No, she wasn't there.'

There was a short pulsing silence. I moistened my lips. 'You mean she hadn't come out? Perhaps the test—'

'No, I mean she wasn't at school at all. I waited for a while and then one of the other girls said she hadn't been there today. So I—I rang to see if she was ill.'

I said carefully, 'But of course she was there. I didn't want her to go, but she insisted because of the French test.' There was an awkward silence and I added uncertainly, 'Perhaps the girl you spoke to was in another class and just didn't happen to see her.'

'No.' Mark's voice sounded shaken but sure of his facts. 'It was Rebecca Forrest who told me. She has the next desk to Briony. Apparently they were all surprised when she didn't turn up, because she'd been working hard for that test.'

The breeze from the open window rippled across my bare wet shoulders and I shivered. 'I don't understand,' I said numbly.

'Shall I get my bike out and have a scout round? Perhaps she felt faint and sat down to rest somewhere.'

'Would you, Mark? Thank you.' I put the phone down and stood staring at the moisture clouding it from my damp hand.

Behind me Lance's voice said sharply. 'Was that Briony?'

I turned slowly. 'No, it was Mark. He says she hasn't been at school today.'

'Hasn't—? But that's ridiculous. She insisted, because of—'

'Yes, I know.'

We stared at each other across the room, each afraid to move lest the hovering cloud of

87

fear and apprehension should swoop down and engulf us. I said, 'He's going out on his bike to look for her.'

'To look where, for Pete's sake?'

I shook my head blindly, clutching at the towel.

'You'd better get some clothes on. You'll catch a chill.'

'What time did she leave the house? About eight-thirty? *Someone* must have seen her, children going to school or someone hurrying for a train to work.'

'Eight-thirty. That's about nine hours. She was all right when she left here. If she didn't go to school, where the hell did she go?'

'I don't know.' The trembling had started and I fought to control it. 'Suppose on the way she decided after all she couldn't face the test. What would she be most likely to do?'

'Come back here, I should have thought.'

'She might not have wanted to worry us.'

'This is ten times worse.'

'Mark said she might have felt faint and sat down to rest somewhere.'

'For eight hours?' His voice cracked. 'If only she'd let me take her in the car as I suggested. I should have insisted.'

If only. How many times had those sad little words been whispered in an agony of self-reproach? If only I'd done that, or not done something else. If only—if only.

My teeth were chattering. Lance took my

88

dressing-gown off the back of the door and brought it over, exchanging it for the damp towel. I said, 'I'll ring Rebecca first and find out what I can.'

But Rebecca merely repeated what she had told Mark. To their surprise, Briony had never arrived at school, and as far as she knew no one had seen her on the way there. My legs gave way and I sat down shakily on the bed. 'Did she take her bicycle?' I asked Lance, who was still hovering at my side.

'I'll go and see.' He seemed glad to have something definite to do. Envying him, I sat unmoving. Minutes later he was back. 'No, it's in the garage.'

'Then she either walked or took the bus.'

'She said something about wanting some fresh air.'

'Suppose she walked then. How far is it to the school? About a mile?'

'Along the road, yes, but if she hadn't got her bike she would probably have cut across the fields. That would explain why no one saw her.'

Across the fields. The words rang in my head like a knell. Might some strange, sick person have been waiting in the fields for a pretty girl to come along?

Lance said abruptly, 'I'll get the car out and comb the side streets. If that doesn't do any good, I'll walk across the fields and see if there's any trace of her.'

'I'll come with you.'

'No. First get dressed, then ring everyone you can think of whom she might have called to see. Anyone she's ever mentioned. And try to keep calm. She could still walk in at any moment, wondering what all the fuss is about.'

But suppose the Other One had intruded into Briony's troubled consciousness? Suppose without Mark's restraining influence this unknown entity had really taken Briony away? What would it do with her?

'Ann! Did you hear what I said?'

'Yes.'

'Then do as I say, there's a good girl. I'll get back as soon as I can and if there's any news I'll phone at once.' He looked at me doubtfully for a moment but I couldn't speak, and he went out of the room. I heard him run down the stairs, the slam of the front door and minutes later the car engine. Eventually, cautiously, I stood up and began automatically to get dressed, carefully holding my mind above the abyss of terror which waited just beneath the surface. First I'd phone the Pomfretts, then Cynthia, then—

Half an hour later when Lance returned, I was still hopelessly phoning. A quick glance at each other's face was all that was needed to tell us there was still no news. It was now six o'clock and we could no longer pretend that she might walk in at any moment. It was Lance who put our joint decision into words.

'We'd better phone the police.' I watched

him start to dial but my ears were closed to what he said. 'They don't seem to regard it as serious under twenty-four hours,' he said testily when he put down the phone. 'Say she might have decided to go to the cinema or something. You'd think they'd give us credit for knowing she'd never do that without letting us know.'

'But she might, Lance,' I said through dry lips. 'She's not herself at the moment.' Then who was she? The question leapt out at me and I winced at its impact.

'They also asked if there was a suitcase missing or anything in her room that might give us a lead. Have you looked in there?'

I shook my head. Together we went across the landing. Briony's room was in its usual happy chaos—laddered tights on the floor, letters strewn over the dressing-table.

'Where does she keep her case?'

'Up there.' I nodded to the top of the wardrobe. The lid of the suitcase was plainly visible. It was ludicrous even to consider that she might have taken it. She wasn't running away, for goodness sake—was she?

Lance had moved over to the desk by the window and begun opening drawers at random. 'What are these?'

Something in his voice dragged my attention back and I went quickly towards him. He was holding a sheaf of rather stiff white paper and on the top sheet was a sketch of the house—

surprisingly good.

'Perhaps she really is interested in taking up art,' I suggested. He did not reply. He turned over the next sheet and to my alarm swayed suddenly. I caught his arm, holding on to the paper which his shaking hand was agitating violently. A girl's face gazed up at us, wide-eyed, mischievous, framed in a cloud of waving hair. To the right of the wide, humorous mouth was a small mole. It was astonishingly life-like. I said unbelievingly, 'Briony drew that? What does it say?' I leant closer. Across the bottom corner was scribbled 'Self Portrait 1958'.

'*Self* portrait? But it doesn't look at all like her. At least—not really. And the date obviously can't be right. She wasn't even born then.'

As I stopped speaking I became conscious of the quality of Lance's silence. His face had taken on a greenish tinge and was gleaming with sweat and the violent shaking which, as my hand released the paper, rattled it ferociously again, had taken hold of his entire body in a merciless series of convulsions.

'What is it, Lance?' I cried stridently. 'Whatever's wrong?'

He dropped the papers and turned away, stumbling to the open window and leaning on the sill to draw in gulps of air. He muttered something in a low voice, more to himself than to me. It sounded like, 'It can't be happening, but it is.'

'What did you say?'

He turned to look at me, bewildered fear in his eyes. 'It's *Briony* we want.'

'Yes darling, I know, but it won't do us any good if you crack up as well.'

He didn't seem to hear me. He said wonderingly, 'Am I going mad, Ann? Is this some sort of revenge?'

I stared back at him, fear lapping over me. 'Lance, please pull yourself together. I need you.' My voice broke. His eyes shuttered and refocused on me. Silently he held out a hand and I ran to him, leaning against him for support. I could feel the heat of his body scorching through the thin shirt and the erratic pounding of his heart. His arms came up suddenly and gripped me painfully, making me gasp for breath, but there was an element of fierce pleasure in the pain. It was the first time I could remember that Lance had seemed to need me as much as I needed him. The moment passed. His arms slackened and I moved away from him.

'There must be *something* we can do,' I said desperately. 'Did you go all the way along the field path?'

'Yes. It's pretty open. She'd have been in full view if she'd fallen or anything.' His voice was jerky, as though he was having to search for the individual words he needed. A tap on the door spun us round to see Mrs Rose standing nervously, her hands plucking at her apron.

93

'Excuse me ma'am, sir, I was wondering what time Miss Briony will be home. Dinner is almost ready.'

Lance answered, 'We don't know, Rosie. Apparently she never arrived at school today. We're very worried about her.'

'Oh mercy!' The woman's face was frightened. Her fingers intensified their compulsive plucking. 'Could she have been kidnapped or something?'

'I don't think that's very likely, but as you know she's not been too well and we're afraid she might be ill somewhere and perhaps—not know where she is.' I looked across at him swiftly. Although I had said nothing to him of my deepest fear, the idea of amnesia had apparently occurred to him too.

'You hear such dreadful things, though,' the housekeeper went on tremblingly. 'Young girls disappear and are sometimes never heard of again. And sometimes, years later—' Her voice faded.

'Yes, well we certainly don't want to think along those lines,' Lance said rallyingly, and I was aware from the twitching muscle in his temple what the effort cost him. 'In the meantime, we all need to keep up our strength, so we must eat even if we don't feel at all like it. Come along, dear.'

He took my arm and led me gently across to the door. Just for a moment his eyes fell to the drawings scattered on the carpet and a tremor passed over his face. Then the three of us, each wrapped in a separate dimension of fear, went shakily downstairs to the waiting, unwanted meal.

CHAPTER SIX

The next forty-eight hours were of unremitting strain and fear. As hour slid into hour I had to fight an increasing hopelessness which began invidiously to pervade my thoughts. Resolutely I kept telling myself that if in truth Briony had simply 'gone away'—mentally as well as physically—then sooner or later she would 'come back' and realise who she was. And whenever that happened, she would surely phone us. In anticipation of this call I refused to undress that first night, lying on top of the bed beneath the quilt so as to be ready to leave the house at a moment's notice. In the next bed I knew that Lance too lay unsleeping.

In the morning a policeman called round and took notes of all we could tell him, including Briony's headaches and her blackout the other evening. A house to house search was initiated and to my numb horror I could see groups of men systematically searching the fields opposite, veering away from the narrow path Briony would have followed to scour the nearby copses and drag the stream. Outhouses were searched, enquiries made at the bus depot and railway station.

Various tantalising facts emerged which might or might not have to do with her. The clerk at the station booking office knew her by sight and was adamant that he hadn't seen her that morning, but the bus company couldn't be so sure. Different drivers and conductors knew different members of the public and of course the time we were trying to check on was one of the busiest of the day. There *had* been a girl roughly answering to Briony's description who had boarded a bus to Newmarket, but there was no saying whether or not it was actually she and in any case no one had noticed at which stop she left the bus. There appeared to be no further trace of her. Briony looked old enough not to arouse suspicion by the mere fact of not being at school, and in the summer the sixth form girls were allowed to wear their own cotton dresses, so there was no uniform to recognise.

It was Wednesday, and Lance should have been at the art college. He had phoned to explain his absence, cutting short all expressions of consternation and sympathy at the other end of the line. 'I have to be with my wife,' he'd repeated more than once. I was touched by his thoughtfulness but as the gruelling day wore on, I found myself wishing passionately that I could be alone. His tangible anxiety, his starting every time the phone rang, intensified my own reactions to the point where I had to bear everything in double measure.

At one point I slipped away from him up to Briony's bedroom and sat looking about me as though some clue might be written in the wallpaper. I bent to gather up the scattered drawings and studied them more closely. I couldn't imagine what it was about them that had triggered off Lance's violent reaction. They were very good—I could see that. Several were of the same girl who had been labelled 'Self Portrait'—mostly unfinished sketches with the head turned in different directions. But one group of figures seemed vaguely familiar and I realised with a sense of shock that they resembled preliminary sketches for a section of the painting downstairs. Immediately all the old fear and distrust welled up in me again. I had always hated Briony's absorption with it. On the other hand, what could be more natural, if the girl really wanted to paint, than to experiment in reproducing a work of her father's which she so obviously admired?

Morning slid into afternoon. In desperation for something to occupy me, I burst into the office. Startled, Moira looked up, her rather austere face softening when she saw mine.

'For pity's sake give me something to do,' I said hoarsely.

'Of course. Perhaps you'd check these sheets of figures with me?'

I was glad to. It passed two full hours. Lance looked in once to see where I was, hung around for a few minutes and then went out again. By the time I came to the end of the task the figures had blurred into wicked black little men wriggling and climbing over the paper, but they had served their purpose.

There were one or two false alarms. The police phoned to say Briony had been reported in Aldeburgh and again later in Cambridge. After hours of unbearable tension, both sightings were discounted. At regular intervals Mrs Rose brought in cups of tea, bowls of soup, sandwiches. My throat was blocked with a knot of solid nauseous fear. Lance, too, pushed the food away from him untouched. By nine o'clock that evening I was completely exhausted.

'I think I'll go upstairs and have a bath,' I said.

'Yes, all right.' He hesitated. 'Would you mind if I went to the studio for a while? You can ring me on the internal phone if you need me.'

'Yes, you go. It might help you to relax.' As always we were as polite to each other as strangers. Apart from that desperate brief straining together in Briony's room, our joint agony had done nothing to bring us closer. Wearily I made my way upstairs. The evening was warm, the air outside still purple. I lay back in the scented water drifting in and out of sleep until the coolness round my thighs forced me out of the bath. I had intended to spend the night fully dressed again, but the waiting garments looked confining and uncomfortable. Instead I just slipped on my dressing-gown. I could dress quickly enough when—if—Briony phoned.

I laid my clothes carefully on a chair so that I could put them on with maximum speed. Then, in the cool loose robe I lay down—just for a minute—on the bed.

I woke with a start some hours later. I had been dreaming Lance was calling me and I was unable to get to him. Had it been a warning? My mind was in a state to believe any fantasy. The room was in darkness. I switched on the light and, blinking, looked at the bedside clock. One-thirty. And Lance's bed was still untouched. The dream swooped back, closing over me with superstitious dread. I slipped off the bed, pushed my feet into slippers and pulled the belt of my robe tighter. Then I opened the door and stood on the landing listening. All was quiet and still. Mrs Rose, knowing Lance was still in the studio, had left a small lamp burning for him in the sitting-room to guide him across the dark garden. Its pale glow barely reached the hall but was sufficient for me to make my way down the stairs.

The long shadowed room lay still. The small yellow pool lit only the corner by the french windows. Silently as a burglar I crossed the room and let myself soundlessly out on to the moonlit terrace. Over to my right a tree rustled suddenly and my heart leapt. No light was streaming across the grass from the studio. In a rush of panic I sped down the steps and over the soaking dew-wet grass, round the corner to the studio. It was lit only by the moonlight. I said 'Lance!' but the word didn't leave my throat. Then I saw him. He was lying halfway across the table beside the easel, his head buried in his arms. Fear deluged me. First Briony, now—

'*Lance!*' I said again, and this time my voice rang through the silent room. To my boundless relief he spun round, staring up at me. In the moonlight I could see traces of tears on his ravaged face. I said on a sob, 'Oh, darling!' and as I moved forward he reached out blindly and grabbed hold of me, pulling me towards him. I stood for a long time pressing his head against my body and as the robe gaped open, felt his hot wet tears on my skin. Time had no meaning. I simply cradled his shaking shoulders, my cheek resting on the thick fair hair. After a while he grew quieter but his grip didn't ease and at last, slowly, still holding me, he rose to his feet. I stood motionless, waiting. Gently he raised his hands and slipped the open robe off my shoulders. It fell to the ground in a rustling heap.

'Ann,' he said softly. I reached up to cup his face with my hands and drew it down to mine.

The sky was already paling when we made our way back across the grass, and the light of the faithful little lamp was swallowed up in the grey of dawn. Lance switched it off as we passed. Back up the stairs we went, leaving two sets of wet footprints on the carpet. In the bedroom he tilted back my chin and looked searchingly down into my face. I put my hand up over his and he smiled a little ruefully.

'Not much of a helpmate, am I? Just when you need me most I fold, and you have to play the role of comforter.'

Since I couldn't find the words to describe how I felt I made no reply. This would have been the most wonderful night of my life, if only Briony were safely home. But if she had been, the situation would never have arisen.

It was nine o'clock before we woke, and the night hours had no more substance than a faintly remembered dream. Once more we were edgy, full of dread, straining for the sound of the telephone. Another day like yesterday. I knew, especially after last night, that I couldn't bear it. As we ate our belated breakfast I urged Lance to go to college as usual.

'I shan't leave the house,' I promised, 'and if there's any news you'll have it as soon as I do. Yesterday we only made each other worse—you must see that. You need to get away from this atmosphere for a few hours, to have something else to think about.'

He hesitated and I knew he was tempted. He

was slightly constrained as he always was after our times together. It would be a relief to him to be away from me for a few hours. 'But what about you? What will you do?'

'I'll be all right.'

'I shan't be able to concentrate.'

'Never mind, it will do you good to try.'

Perversely, when he finally gave in and went out to the car, I almost called him back. Could I really face another endless day of waiting, all alone?

At ten-thirty I phoned the police station, without hope. They were kind and reassuring. No, there was no news as yet but there were several promising leads they were following up. After the disappointment of yesterday they didn't want to go into details until more definite information was to hand. As soon as they had any—

Wearily I put the phone down. Moira wasn't here today so there were no more figures to check. Mrs Rose had her transistor turned down low, as befitted a house of mourning. Swiftly I repudiated the phrase. My straining ears could just detect the cheerful, inconsequential prattle of a disc jockey. If she derived any comfort from his banalities I could not grudge it to her.

At lunch time she brought me the inevitable bowl of soup. My throat closed at the sight of it. Yet somehow I must keep my strength up. 'I think perhaps,' I said gently, 'I might manage one very small, fluffy omelette, if you wouldn't mind making one. I—seem awash with soup!'

'Of course, madam.'

But when it came the omelette was after all beyond me. I managed a bare half of it, choking it down against the threat of nausea. The morning paper still lay in its pristine folds on the coffee table. I picked it up and put it down again, moving restlessly about the room. And with the compulsion of a magnet the painting drew me unwillingly towards it. Dully my eyes went over the exquisite colours, the ethereal quality which had led more than one enthusiastic critic to compare it with the work of Hieronymous Bosch.

Well, I addressed it silently, are you satisfied now? Is this what you wanted, to drive her away from us? No doubt it was neurotic to hold an inanimate work of art to blame, but in fact it seemed to have a mind, a dimension, very much its own. It withstood my confrontation stoically and I turned helplessly away. Yet conversely I was left with a thread of comfort. There was an undeniable psychic bond of some kind between Briony and the painting. Eventually she would have to return to it.

I put my hands to my throbbing head. The constant stress was obviously addling my brain. If only there were someone other than the respectfully sombre Mrs Rose to talk to! And, like the answer to a prayer, Edgar came.

103

He stood hesitantly just inside the door, uncertain of his welcome, with the same half-hopeful, half-cautious expression on his face with which I had so often seen him await Cynthia. And he said deprecatingly, 'If you'd rather I just left, you only have to say so.'

I had taken a couple of steps towards him before I remembered the ambiguity of our last meeting and stopped dead, torn by conflicting emotions. Then I said helplessly, 'Oh, Edgar!' and burst into tears. All the mounting worry and dread of the last few days, capped by the frenzy of Lance's love-making and his inevitable withdrawal that morning, was suddenly more than I could stand. I had never been so emotionally vulnerable in my life. I just stood like a child, sobbing uncontrollably with my hands over my face and Edgar came swiftly across and took me in his arms, holding me close and murmuring words of comfort as, not so many hours before, I had held Lance. I was in desperate need of someone to lean on, someone who, in the face of this particular trouble, was not weaker than I was myself. Edgar supplied that need and asked for no repayment. Not then.

'I thought at least Lance would have been with you,' he said when my sobs had quietened to a series of gentle hiccups, and the anger in his voice comforted me further, even though it was unwarranted.

'I persuaded him to go to college,' I

murmured, fumbling for a handkerchief. Edgar put his own into my groping hand. It was large and soft and smelt of tobacco. I said between a laugh and a sob, 'I'd better not get lipstick on it, or you'll have some explaining to do!'

'It wouldn't matter to Cynthia,' he replied quietly, and then, abruptly closing that line of conversation, '*Why* did you persuade him to go to college?'

I dabbed ineffectually at my eyes. 'Because he's so desperately worried himself he makes me worse.'

Edgar's arms tightened fractionally and I felt the time had come to disengage myself. This I did, gently, and he made no attempt to prevent my moving away.

'Thanks for providing a shoulder, Edgar. I really needed that.'

'If you can talk about it all, tell me exactly what happened.'

He sat down beside me on the couch and took hold of my hand. It seemed a natural gesture with no intention other than continued comfort, and I let my hand lie in his. Carefully omitting all the queries which loomed so large in my mind and, I was beginning to suspect, even large in Lance's, I said merely that Briony's headaches had been causing us concern for some time and we were afraid that she had unknowingly suffered from one or two attacks of amnesia. This seemed the most probable explanation of her disappearance.

'The police called at the house yesterday, making enquiries,' he told me. 'It's something you hear about all the time, but you never dream of it happening to you.'

'No,' I said numbly

'So all you can do is wait?' I nodded, not trusting my voice. 'I suppose there's some comfort in the fact that you've an idea what might have happened. At least there's a possible explanation other than—' He broke off with an anxious sideways glance at my set face.

'Murderers lurking in the bushes,' I finished for him. 'Yes, I suppose you're right. I'm quite sure she'd never accept a lift in a car, because we've drummed that into her ever since she was tiny.'

We sat in silence for a while, busy with our thoughts. At one point I said, 'Shouldn't you be at work?'

'I'm visiting a client,' he answered with a faint smile. 'Actually, I have visited one, and no one's checking up to see how long it took me to get back to the office. I just wanted to pop in and see how you were. As I said, I thought Lance would be here.' He paused. 'I can imagine he would go to pieces if anything happened to Briony.'

It might have been my over-active imagination, but his faint stressing of the last word managed to convey a host of things he

106

could never say outright. Even so, I resented it and childishly removed my hand from his. 'I'll ask Mrs Rose to make some tea. Poor woman, she's hardly done anything else for the last— how long is it? It seems weeks, but I suppose it's still only two days.'

'How's Lance getting on with Stella?' Edgar asked as we sat drinking it. 'Has he started painting her yet?'

'She's only had one sitting. She's due again tomorrow. I suppose I'd better put her off. That is, unless—'

'Cynthia was saying Stella seemed more concerned about missing her hair appointment than anything else!' He put down his cup and saucer. 'I suppose I really ought to be going, but—'

'I'm all right now, Edgar,' I said quickly. 'You came at exactly the right moment and I'm very grateful. Don't worry about me.'

'I do worry about you, though. No one else seems to.' Again the implied criticism of Lance.

I said wryly, 'I do enough worrying on my own account to exonerate everyone else! Really, though, I'm much better now. I suppose I'd been bottling things up.' I stood up and he did the same. He started to move towards me but I slipped past him and led the way to the door. 'Give my love to Cynthia,' I added, less than sincerely. He nodded, hesitated, and then, with a little pat on my arm, walked out of the front door. I was still

107

watching him drive away when the phone rang. 'Yes? Hello?'

An infuriating buzz, a click, and then, rather faintly, a man's voice, with a strong Scottish accent. 'Would that be Mrs Tenby speaking?'

I felt the sweat break out from every pore of my body. Ransom demand? Some distant hospital reporting an accident? 'Yes?'

'I'm not hearing you very well.'

I raised my voice. 'This is Mrs Tenby. Who's that?'

'Rutherbrae Police Station, Glasgow, ma'am. We have your daughter here.'

Everything swam in an eddying circle. I gripped the phone and closed my eyes tight.

'Hello? Mrs Tenby?'

'Yes, I—I did hear you. Is she all right?'

'She's a wee bit confused, seemingly. Would you like a word with her?'

'Oh, please!' She was safe! Briony was safe! Everything would be all right now. And then came the hesitant voice across all those miles.

'Mother?'

'Oh darling, thank God!' I fought for control. 'Are you all right?'

'I seem to be.' Her voice shook. 'I don't know what happened.'

'Never mind that, sweetheart. You stay there at the police station and we'll come up on the first available plane and collect you.'

'Please hurry.' The break was in her voice again.

108

'We'll be with you in a few hours.'

Tremblingly I replaced the phone and turned to see Mrs Rose hovering in the kitchen doorway, hope struggling with disbelief on her face.

'It was Briony!' I said jubilantly. 'She's all right. We're going to collect her straight away.'

'Oh, ma'am.' The poor soul's lips were quivering. 'I'm so—'

I nodded to show that I understood and she turned back into the kitchen, quietly shutting the door. Spontaneously I dropped to my knees, bowed my head, and said to anyone who might be listening, 'Thank you. Oh, thank you, thank you, thank you!'

It wasn't until I phoned Lance and, after his first joyful exclamation, he repeated incredulously, 'She's in *Scotland*?' that the full impact hit me. It was to the country which she loved but had hysterically refused to visit that Briony's alter ego had taken her. Somehow, I knew fearfully that this was of tremendous significance.

CHAPTER SEVEN

My forebodings increased when, minutes later as I was quickly packing an overnight bag, Lance returned home and came up the stairs two at a time.

'I couldn't ask any questions on the phone—I was in the principal's study—but tell me everything now. Whereabouts is she?'

'At a place called Rutherbrae. I think he said it was Glasgow.'

Lance's face froze. '*Rutherbrae*?'

'Yes. Why?' I gazed at him apprehensively. After a moment he said tonelessly, 'I had a flat there when I was at art school.'

'Perhaps you mentioned it some time and she subconsciously remembered it.'

'I'm damn sure I didn't. We just thought of it as Glasgow. Why the hell she should have chosen that particular—'

'We don't know that she did choose it, Lance,' I reminded him quietly.

'No.' He moved his tongue over his lips. 'How did she seem?'

'Confused, according to the police. She said she didn't know what had happened.'

'Have you phoned the airport to book a flight?'

'There's no need now there's the shuttle service. There are planes every hour or so and we get the tickets actually on board. All we have to do is catch the first flight we can.'

He stood irresolutely in the middle of the room. I said, 'Have you enough petrol to get us to Heathrow?'

'Yes, luckily I filled her up this morning.'

'I've packed your night things and a clean shirt. We might as well go straight away, then.'

110

I noticed with concern that there was sweat on his forehead. 'Are you feeling all right, Lance?'

'Yes, yes, fine.' He brushed the question impatiently aside. 'She's not hurt in any way?'

'I don't think so.'

'Has she been up there all the time?'

'I've no idea. We'll have to be careful not to overwhelm her with questions.' I steered him gently in the direction of the door and followed with the case. 'Mrs Rose, will you phone Mrs Pomfrett and cancel the sitting for tomorrow? And perhaps you'd also ring Mrs Pemberton and Mrs Staveley to let them know Briony's safe and we're going to bring her home.'

'Yes, of course. What time shall I expect you back, ma'am?'

'We probably won't want to be up too early in the morning. I should think we'll catch a plane about lunch time and be home between four and five. It takes longer to get to Suffolk from Heathrow than to fly from Glasgow!'

I was marvelling at my regained control. Lance seemed incapable of taking command. I wondered a little impatiently why he was still so pale and drawn now that we knew Briony was safe.

We drove almost in silence to the airport. Every now and then Lance would ask a question which I answered as best I could. For the rest he concentrated almost entirely on driving, his face set and withdrawn. The remembered closeness there had been between

111

us the previous night only emphasised the vast distances separating us now. He had turned blindly to me in Briony's absence. Now she was coming home. I had served my purpose; he had no further need of me. Unwisely I found myself remembering the comforting shelter of Edgar's arms and hastily shuttered the memory away. It was no use being bitter and full of self-pity. Lance had never promised to love me. His love was entirely for Briony and he had made the fact clear from the very first.

Heathrow was a moving morass of people, of jostling porters with trolleys, of luggage and disembodied voices booming across the huge spaces.

'You'd better arrange to hire a car the other end,' I said practically. He turned into a phone booth and began to leaf through the lists of car hire firms. He dialled, spoke for a few minutes, and rejoined me. Close together but untouching we moved with the stream in the direction we'd been shown. The evening was cloudy and warm and London lay grey and listless as we climbed steeply, the beating pulse of the city undetectable from this altitude. It seemed we had hardly straightened out into level flight before the note of the engines changed again as we started the long descent.

Renfrew, too, was cloudy and slightly less warm. The hired car awaited us and with the minimum of formalities we were driving again, past buildings of grey stone, dull and

112

colourless after the pastel shades of Suffolk. Was it really only a week since I'd had tea with Jan and told her of my meeting with Lance? I had little imagined that I should be in Scotland again so soon.

'Do we have to go through the city centre to reach Rutherbrae?' I asked.

'No, it's on this side of town.' His face was white and shining, his lower lip in shreds where he had been chewing it. He said, almost under his breath, 'Twenty years, and it's hardly changed at all.'

We found the police station without any difficulty since it was opposite the bus terminus. As we went inside, Lance clutching my elbow, the duty sergeant glanced up and came round the desk to meet us.

'Mr and Mrs Tenby?'

'Yes. Where is she?'

'She's lying down just now, sir. If you'll take a seat I'll send a woman police constable to fetch her.'

'Lying down?'

'She was still a mite distressed. The police doctor gave her a sedative.'

Moments later a fresh-faced woman in uniform appeared leading Briony by the arm. She looked half asleep. Her hair was tousled and the crisp cotton dress in which she had set out for school on Tuesday morning was dirty and creased. She caught sight of us, and I saw her eyes widen as they rested on Lance, with a

113

wild, questioning uncertainty. Then he had moved swiftly forward and caught her into his arms. Over his shoulder the white disc of her face still retained an expression of puzzled anxiety. She gently extricated herself and came into my arms. I could feel her trembling. She said haltingly, 'Mother, I'm sorry. You must have been frantic. I just don't know—'

'Hush, darling, it doesn't matter now. We've plenty of time to sort it all out.'

The routine for releasing her into our care was duly completed and we drove straight to the Lanark Hotel. It was large and impersonal and catered mainly for businessmen. We were able without any trouble to book a double and a single room with a communicating bathroom, and as soon as the porter had left us Briony lay down on one of the beds and closed her eyes. Lance watched her anxiously.

'Do you feel like telling us everything you can remember?'

'It won't take long. I hardly remember a thing.' Her lip quivered and she caught it quickly between her teeth. Lance sat on the bed beside her and took her hand. I stayed unmoving by the dressing-table, watching them both.

'I remember saying good-bye to you in the dining-room, and hoping the sitting with Mrs Pomfrett would go well. And—that's it.' Her eyes were still shut, but slow tears were seeping beneath the lids.

'What about leaving the house?' Lance prompted gently. 'Can you remember that?'

'Vaguely. Yes—because I passed the postman in the drive and asked if there was anything for me. I'd forgotten that bit.'

'There, you see, your memory's starting to come back already.'

She shook her head hopelessly.

'Try again, sweetheart. Did you go to Rushyford along the main road or across the fields?'

'I don't know. Really I don't.'

'Do you remember catching a bus?'

'No, I wanted some fresh air.'

'And you've no recollection at all of what happened next?'

'*No*, Daddy.' She paused, then added in a poignant little whisper, 'Please don't keep asking me. I've tried so hard to remember.'

'What's the next thing you can remember?' I asked.

'Standing in a strange street this afternoon. Quite literally that. In fact, I was looking in a shop window. I could see tubes of paint and brushes laid out and my own face reflected in the glass. And for one utterly horrifying moment I didn't recognise myself. I didn't look as I *expected* to look.' She drew a deep, steadying breath and opened her tear-filled eyes. 'Then almost at once I remembered, and at first I was so thankful to know *who* I was that it didn't seem to matter *where*. When I found

115

out I was in Scotland I just couldn't believe it. I had been so against coming, and to find that I'd come in spite of myself—well, that really was creepy. It was as though I'd no longer any control over what I wanted to do.' She looked up suddenly. 'The policeman told me it's *Thursday.*'

She was begging for reassurance but we could only nod confirmation.

'Then where have I been since I left home?' Her voice rose. 'Where did I spend last night? And Tuesday night? It's just—ludicrous! I can't suddenly *lose* two whole days like that!'

'It'll come back gradually, dear,' I soothed, with more conviction than I felt. 'You've already remembered about seeing the postman.' But that might actually have been her last moment as Briony Tenby before she slipped into—whom? Briefly I wondered if anything might be gained from questioning the postman. He might even have seen the change-over without realising it. But if such a drastic split had indeed occurred, it might be better if she never recovered the memory. Again I caught the flicker in her eyes as she looked up at Lance.

I said with an effort, 'I don't suppose any of us has eaten much in the last few days. It's nearly eight-thirty. I suggest we go down for dinner and then all have an early night.'

I don't remember much about the meal. Anti-climax had settled over me with a

116

suffocating pall and I was tired to the point of disintegration. The succession of sleepless nights and all the turmoil of the waking hours lay heavily on my eyelids. I had the greatest difficulty in stifling my yawns. The only incident during dinner that does remain in my mind is Briony's sudden query: 'Didn't we come here once with Mac?'

The glass in Lance's hand jerked violently and a red stain spread down the front of his jacket. I asked as naturally as I could, 'Mac who? I don't remember being here before.'

Lance said nothing at all. After a moment Briony replied, 'I must have dreamt it. It just suddenly seemed to ring a bell.' We both looked at Lance but he didn't meet our eyes. The pulse was beating insistently in his temple. Soon after that we went upstairs. I had intended to have a bath but was now so sleepy I decided to postpone it till the morning. I was already in bed and Lance was brushing his teeth in the bathroom when Briony, barefoot and in the nightdress I'd brought for her, came through to our room.

I sat up. 'What is it, dear?'

She said in a small voice, 'Can I sleep in here, with you? I'm frightened of being alone, in case I—go away again. I can sleep on a chair or anything, just as long as I can stay.'

Lance said firmly, 'You're certainly not sleeping in a chair, and nor is anyone else. If you want to stay here you can have my bed and

117

I'll use yours.'

'But I don't want to turn you out—Daddy.' Only I seemed to register the slight hesitation before his name.

'Nonsense. Now in you get and straight off to sleep. We've a busy day again tomorrow, travelling home.' He looked across at me. 'Good-night, Ann. Sleep well.' He closed the bathroom door behind him. Briony looked at me.

'Sorry, Mother.'

'It's all right, darling. I'm happier keeping an eye on you, anyway.' And Lance was obviously relieved to be away from both of us for a few hours. She bent down to kiss me and climbed into the adjacent bed. I reached up to switch off the light and blessed darkness at last brought an end to the chaotic, turbulent day.

I woke the next morning to the unfamiliar sound of footsteps overhead and the muted hum of heavy traffic. Alongside me Briony still slept heavily. For a while I lay reviewing the still unsolved problems which surrounded us and eventually, when it was obvious sleep would not return, I went through for my postponed bath. Above the running water I thought I caught the sound of voices from behind the door leading to Lance's room, and after my bath I tapped on it and went in. He was sitting up in bed reading *The Scotsman*, a cup of tea on the table beside him.

'I thought I heard sounds. How did you sleep?'

'So-so.' He laid down the paper. 'Is Briony awake?'

'She wasn't when I came through for my bath.'

'I've just been on to the police again, to see if they could tell us any more than she could.'

'And did they?' I closed the door softly behind me.

'Not a great deal. Apparently she approached a policeman in the street early yesterday afternoon and told him she didn't know where she was or how she'd got there. She was in what they called a "distressed condition". He radioed for assistance and they came in a police car and took her back to the station. That was when they phoned you.'

'Was she near your flat?' I asked with studied casualness.

His face twitched slightly. 'Yes, just in the next road. The shop she described sounds like the one where we used to get some of our supplies.'

'It could only have been coincidence, though, couldn't it?'

'Search me. Ann, what are we going to do about her?' Anxiety was strident in his voice. 'There must be something seriously wrong.'

'I know.' I sat on the edge of the bed. 'I can't think why she came here when she was so against coming to Scotland. Could the art

119

school have any particular significance for her?'

If the idea had not been so ridiculous, I would have sworn that the expression which flickered in his eyes was sheer naked fear. 'How could it?' His voice was almost unrecognisable.

'I don't know, except that she seems to have become interested in painting herself, and since she thinks so much of you, she might subconsciously have decided to come here herself.'

'I suppose it's just possible. The thing I find most unnerving is that she came all this way *without knowing it.*'

'Yes.' I couldn't elaborate on the half-formed thoughts which fluttered so distortedly in my mind. I said with an effort, 'Possibly the severity of the headaches brought on some kind of amnesia and her subconscious just took over. To understand that, we'd have to consult a psychiatrist.' I held my breath, and as I'd expected his reaction was swift.

'No, thank you! I'm not having any of those pseudo-psycho fellows messing about with her. Burton's a sound man, he'll know what to do.'

'He did mention psychoanalysis himself,' I began diffidently.

'When?'

'The last time we saw him, after she'd passed out. He couldn't find any orthodox medical reason for the attacks. All the tests and X-rays they did last month were negative.'

120

'I thought no one knew the causes of migraine?'

'I doubt if migraine as such could lead to actual amnesia.'

'It might. Anyway, she was due to see Burton again this week, wasn't she? We'd better have him round as soon as we get her home.'

The door from the bathroom opened behind me and Briony stood there rubbing her eyes. 'I thought you must have gone down for breakfast.'

I stood up. 'Not without telling you, but now you're awake we might as well all get dressed.'

'Briony—' The note in Lance's voice halted us and we turned back. 'Has anything like this ever happened before? To a lesser degree, of course, but—things happening without you being aware of them?'

Remembering what Jan had said I waited anxiously, but her reply was vague and indecisive. 'I don't think so, though sometimes things do seem rather blurred when I look back. I suppose everyone finds that.'

We neither confirmed nor denied it. I suspected that few people 'went away' when out for the evening, meanwhile managing to bypass a very real allergy. But perhaps allergies were basically 'in the mind' and the one who took over from Briony simply hadn't been aware of her antipathy to shrimps. Would that be sufficient lack of stimulus for her body not to react? Only Max Forrest could answer me.

121

I thought increasingly of Max throughout the tensions of the long journey home. Briony was subdued but I was actually more worried about Lance, whose persistent pallor made him look drawn and ill. Did he perhaps have some inkling what all this was about, something that was so grotesque he did not dare to begin to accept it? It began to look as though he too was in need of analysis.

It was almost four when we eventually reached home. Briony was exhausted and while I helped her undress and get into bed, Lance phoned Dr Burton. He promised to call at the house before evening surgery. The sketches which had had such an effect on Lance lay neatly on top of the desk in Briony's room where I had laid them.

'Did you do these, darling?' I asked casually as she was brushing her hair. She glanced across, hesitated, then looked up at me.

'I—think so. That's one of the things I'm a bit hazy about.'

'They're extremely good. I just wondered why most of them seem to be of the same girl, and who she is?'

'I don't know who she is,' she answered slowly, staring at her reflection in the glass as she continued her steady brushing.

'At first I think I was attempting a self portrait. It was really just a means of finding out whether I actually did have any talent in that direction. I—sat down here at the

122

dressing-table and started to draw my reflection.' She frowned a little. 'I don't know quite why it turned out like that. And after that first time, it seemed as though I had to go on drawing the same face, from different angles.'

'Have you any idea,' I asked softly, 'why you called this one "Self Portrait 1958"?'

She stopped brushing. 'No,' she whispered after a moment.

'It was rather a curious thing to do,' I persisted gently. She twisted on the stool to face me.

'But it *was* supposed to be a self portrait originally. I suppose that's why I wrote it. As for the date, it was probably just a slip of the hand—a five instead of a seven.' From the intensity with which she held my eyes, I sensed that she was willing me to accept this.

'I see,' I said casually, turning to replace the sheets on the desk. 'The one of the house is very good, too.' I could actually feel some of the tension drain out of her. Now was not the time to broach with her the possibility of seeing Max. She was still reeling from the traumatic discovery that there were two whole days of her life she had no way of accounting for.

Dr Burton was calm and reassuring, managing to give the impression that nothing very out of the ordinary had happened. He read the note from the Scottish police doctor and nodded agreement. 'I think it would be wise to continue the sedation for tonight as

123

well. If I write out a prescription, perhaps Mr Tenby could take it to the chemists before they close.'

As Lance took the form and left with it, I wondered whether the doctor had deliberately removed him in order to have a private word with me. Sure enough, on the way downstairs he began quietly, 'The last few days seem to have been a severe strain on your husband, Mrs Tenby. Understandable, of course, but—'

I said quickly, 'He's working very hard to complete some paintings required for an exhibition. The worry about Briony on top of that—'

'Yes, I see.' We had reached the foot of the stairs and he paused. 'Have you thought any more about psychoanalysis?'

I met his eyes. 'Would you recommend it, doctor?'

'Frankly, yes. I'm at a loss to explain these attacks and there's the chance they might recur with increasing frequency.'

I said hesitantly, 'My husband isn't very happy about the idea.'

'Nevertheless, I'm afraid we've now reached the stage where I don't feel I can accept full responsibility for your daughter's well-being. She needs more specialised help than I can give her. You mentioned Dr Forrest. I would strongly advise you to let him see her as soon as possible.'

'Obviously I have no alternative,' I said quietly.

'Good. If you call at the surgery tomorrow morning there will be a letter for you to take to him. There's no need to wait until then to make an appointment, though.'

'I'll phone straight away,' I promised, and saw his relief. As soon as he had gone and before Lance returned, I hurriedly dialled the Bury number. Max's secretary answered the phone.

'It's Mrs Tenby speaking. Would you please tell Dr Forrest that I'm extremely worried about my daughter and would be grateful if he could see her as soon as possible?'

'Is your daughter a new patient, Mrs Tenby?'

'Yes.'

'Have you a note from your own doctor?'

'I shall have tomorrow, yes.'

'Hold on a moment, please.'

Then Max's voice in my ear. 'Mrs Tenby? I was expecting to hear from you. The girls tell me your daughter has not been at school.'

'She disappeared for two days. She's no idea what happened during that time.'

'I see.'

'How soon can you see her?' Dr Burton's anxiety had infected me and I was now desperate to take her to Max at the earliest opportunity.

'I haven't really a free appointment on Monday, but—'

125

'Oh, please!'

'Very well, Mrs Tenby. If you can bring her along about four-thirty I'll see her then. In the meantime, try to relax.'

I had just replaced the receiver when Lance's car turned into the gateway. With a heavy heart I watched him get out and walk towards me. I had only become aware of his antipathy towards psychiatrists since his confrontation with Max last Sunday. I wondered uneasily if his vehemence was in part a fear of what analysis might reveal. But what terrible secret could he possibly imagine that Briony might be hiding?

CHAPTER EIGHT

The sedation had not worn off by the time Lance and I had our breakfast the next morning. 'You're going into Rushyford as usual?' I asked anxiously.

'Of course. Paul looks forward to his lessons.'

'But you need a rest today as much as Briony does.'

'I'm afraid I shall have to manage without it.'

Out in the hall the telephone rang and he went quickly to answer it. 'Yes? Oh, hello, Stella. Yes, thank you, she's fine. A little tired but otherwise none the worse. It's kind of you to ring. By the way, I'm sorry I had to cancel the sitting. You couldn't possibly manage to come along this afternoon, could you? I really can't afford to get any more behind at this stage. As you know I didn't make much progress last time you were here. Are you sure? If you don't mind it would be a great help. About two-thirty? Thanks very much. I'll see you then.'

He put his head round the door. 'I presume you heard that?'

'Yes.'

'I really must get on with the exhibition work. This week's been a complete write-off, one way or another. Now don't start making objections, Ann! You know painting relaxes me—I'll be perfectly all right. Do you want a lift into Rushyford?'

'No thanks, I'll stay at home till Briony wakes.'

'Right. See you at lunch time.'

At ten o'clock Cynthia phoned, and I repeated all the reassurances Lance had given Stella. Cynthia said hesitantly, 'You'll hardly want us on Sunday, I imagine?'

'Oh yes indeed, business as usual!' I tried to keep my voice light. 'If you don't come Lance will insist on working, and quite honestly he can't keep going much longer at the pace he's forcing.'

'Don't worry, darling. I'll see he relaxes! I'm

the best brow-stroker in the county!'

With a strained smile I turned from the phone to see Mark Staveley coming up the drive with a bunch of flowers in his hand. I opened the door quickly.

'Hello, Mark. I'm awfully sorry, but Briony isn't awake yet.'

'It doesn't matter. Perhaps you'd give her these, with my love.'

'Thank you, she'll be delighted. Will you come in for a moment?'

'If I'm not disturbing you.'

He followed me through the sitting-room and out on to the terrace. The white wooden bench was warm in the sunshine and he sat down beside me, pushing aside the morning paper. 'Mrs Tenby—'

'Yes?'

He flushed. 'I believe Mum told you I was a bit worried about Briony.'

'Yes, she did.' I waited, nerves stretched.

'She turned up in Scotland, I believe.'

'That's right, near Glasgow.'

'I felt that perhaps you ought to know that when she had these—spells, she talked with a faint Scottish accent.'

There was silence, while I waited desperately for the beating wings of panic to subside. 'I just need to rest a wee while.' Sickly I remembered the effect those words had had on Lance the other evening. But why? Was this Scottish accent connected in some macabre way with

Briony's being found near the flat in Rutherbrae? My brain shied sharply away from the first inklings of a possibility which surely couldn't be a possibility at all. Into the lengthening silence came birdsong and the distant shrill barking of a dog.

Mark said anxiously, 'Mum did explain, about what I call her "going away"?'

'Yes.' I moistened my lips. 'But apart from the shrimps she didn't give me any details.'

'I didn't tell her all that much. I really only wanted her to pass on the warning to you.'

'I appreciate that. Can you—could you give me any details now?'

'It's hard to tie down, really. Sometimes I'm not even sure when it's happening because the change is barely noticeable. That is, the—other personality is so like her own. The shrimp business was the most outstanding evidence I had. But sometimes, when we're in a café having tea, she does quick, lightning little sketches of people at the next table on a scrap of paper. They're incredibly good. And—once—she seemed to think I was someone else, too.'

'How do you mean?' My voice sounded cracked.

'She called me "Jamie".'

After a moment, I said, 'Anything else?' The flood of wild, thankful relief which swamped me brought home to me that I was closer than I had imagined to suspecting the impossible. But

129

there could be no possible connection with 'Jamie'.

'Nothing concrete. It was a succession of little things.'

'When was the first time you noticed this?'

'Again, it's hard to say. I mean, she's always been—volatile, hasn't she? At first I just thought it was a sudden change of mood, then gradually I began to realise that there were times when she didn't remember what we'd been talking about from one "mood" to the other. And eventually I was forced to accept the fact that there were times when she actually seemed to be—a different person.'

I noted dispassionately that his hands were gripping the boards of the bench, his knuckles gleaming white against the brown skin.

I told myself I needed all these details to report to Max, but the effect was agonisingly like prodding a particularly sensitive tooth. 'And about how long do these spells last?'

He moved awkwardly. 'They vary. Sometimes it happens so quickly I've hardly had time to register the change before she's—back. I think the longest was about forty-five minutes.'

'But she behaves quite rationally during that time?'

'Oh yes, except that sometimes she seems to be continuing some conversation I don't remember starting. But there's never anything that anyone watching from a distance would notice.'

'Mark?'

Briony's voice behind us made us both jump guiltily and for a moment I wondered how long she'd been standing there. Mark moved quickly towards her and took hold of her hands. I said steadily, 'Would you like anything to eat, dear?'

'No thank you, just coffee.'

'I'll ask Mrs Rose to bring it out here, and some for Mark. If you'll excuse me I'll go out and do the shopping now. I just wanted to wait until you were awake.'

Mark led her gently to the bench and I went inside, passed on the request to Mrs Rose and collected my bag and shopping list. Jack Gifford was working in the front garden, on his knees near the lily pond. He got stiffly to his feet as I backed the mini out of the garage and stood to one side while I reversed and turned towards the gate. As I drove slowly alongside, he touched his ancient cap. 'Glad you've the little lady safe back again, missis.'

'Thank you, Jack.'

The roads were busy as always on a Saturday morning. I had to park some distance from the surgery and walk the rest of the way. The letter was waiting for me as promised in the prescription box. It was addressed firmly to Dr Max Forrest, with a string of initials after the name. Fleetingly I was tempted to open it myself, but it would all be in medical terms, meaningless to me. In any event, Dr Burton had freely admitted that he didn't know what was wrong; I would learn nothing from any spying.

Lance saw the tight yellow rosebuds as soon as he came home and raised his eyebrows interrogatively.

'Mark brought them,' I answered quietly.

'He didn't waste much time, did he?'

'I think he's genuinely fond of her. I wish you wouldn't always be so critical of him. At least he's not scruffy like some of the boys. Lance—' I spoke quickly, really only trying to lead him away from the thorny subject of Mark. 'Did we ever know anyone called Jamie?'

At first, when he didn't reply, I thought he hadn't heard. His back was towards me and I couldn't see his face. I was about to repeat the question when he answered in an odd, breathless voice, 'I did, once. In another existence. Why do you ask?'

'How do you mean, another—?'

'I said why do you ask?'

He turned then, and my mouth went dry at the sight of his ashen face.

'Mark mentioned it,' I stammered, completely off my guard. 'He said Briony sometimes calls him that.'

'Calls *him* Jamie?' I nodded and he gave a harsh laugh. 'Well, well!'

I said with difficulty, 'Lance what is it? You

132

look terrible. Is there—'

'I'm not surprised.' He went quickly to the drinks cabinet and poured himself a neat whisky, draining it in one gulp. As I watched fearfully he poured another. 'Has it ever occurred to you that I might be insane?' he inquired conversationally. I don't think he expected a reply. Certainly he didn't get one. He had moved over to the picture and was standing in front of it while he sipped his second drink. The door opened and Briony came in, still pale but more like her old self.

'Oh, you're both back. Is lunch ready? I didn't have any breakfast and I'm quite hungry now.' Lance hadn't turned and she went over to him, slipping one arm round his neck. 'Admiring my picture?' she asked.

He turned so suddenly that she took a quick step backwards, her eyes widening at his expression.

'*Your* painting?' The words seemed jolted out of him.

'I—I only meant it's my favourite.'

'Yes.' He visibly pulled himself together, rubbed a hand over his face and drew a deep breath. 'Yes, of course.'

I said precariously, 'How was Paul today?'

'Paul? Oh—physically not so good, poor lad. His mother said it was one of his bad days. However, the painting session helped to take his mind off it.' He finished his drink and set the glass down with a little click. 'Let's eat then,

133

shall we? Stella's coming at two-thirty.'

'You're not seeing Mark this afternoon, are you?' I asked Briony in a low voice.

'No, he has a cricket match. In any case, I feel too lazy to do anything but rest today.'

'Good. We'll have a quiet afternoon together, then.'

She and I were in the garden when Stella arrived, her thick corn-coloured hair tied back with a ribbon. 'Earth Mother reporting for duty!' she announced. 'And please use your influence on that man to let me have my hair done on Tuesday or I shall go completely mad.' She paused, looking down at Briony. 'You okay, love?'

'Yes thank you, Mrs Pomfrett.'

'What was the idea of frightening us all like that?'

Lance came round the shrubbery from the studio. 'Hello, Stella. I thought I heard you.'

'Good grief, Lance, what have you been doing to yourself? If anything you look worse than Briony!'

Lance smiled tightly. 'I'm older than she is and anxiety takes more of a toll.' They walked together round the bank and out of sight. Briony spread out a rug and lay face down on it, cushioning her face in her arms. For a long time neither of us spoke. An aeroplane moved lazily over the blue arc of the sky like an outsize bee, its throbbing hum a part of the summer day. I thought Briony was asleep, but she said suddenly, 'Mother, you remember that film we saw last Sunday?'

Alarm signals triggered through my body, but I only said non-committally, 'Yes?'

'The one about reincarnation?'

'So you all said.'

'Do you believe in it?'

'I don't think I like the idea very much.'

'That's not quite the same thing. Do you think there could be anything in it?'

'Why do you ask?'

'Because sometimes I'm absolutely convinced I've lived before, and not all that long ago, either.'

Impossible that so fantastic a conversation should be taking place in the slumberous peace of this summer garden. Even so, I registered that her words came as no surprise. She turned her head sideways to look up at me.

'The signs and symptoms they quoted in that film—most of them have happened to me.'

Which explained her tension that afternoon.

'Did you mention this to anyone?'

'No.'

'Not even Mark?'

'No. I didn't dare put it into words in case it made it more true.'

'But you have done now.'

'Now things have progressed further, and keeping quiet isn't going to stop them.'

After a moment I said, 'What exactly has happened, Briony?'

'I'm not sure.' Her voice shook. 'Sometimes from the way Mark looks at me, I think he's noticed something strange, but he's never mentioned it. I just feel certain that my going to Scotland without even knowing it is tied up with it in some way.'

I said carefully, 'I don't quite see what amnesia has to do with reincarnation. If you *have* been alive before it must obviously have been as someone else, and whereas you might conceivably remember things, I can't see why it should lead to loss of consciousness now.'

'No,' she said after a while, 'you're right. I hadn't thought of that. The past shouldn't really impinge on this existence. Then I understand even less what's been happening.' She shuddered. 'Perhaps Rachel was nearer the truth when she spoke of possession.'

Out there in the hot sun I was suddenly as cold as ice. I said with an effort, 'Her father didn't go along with that, though. And talking of Dr Forrest, he may well be the person to help you.'

'Yes,' she said quietly, 'I'd wondered about that myself.'

'Dr Burton thinks it might be a good idea for you to see him.'

'He's washed his hands of me, has he?'

'Of course not, but he doesn't think he can be of enough help. As a matter of fact I've made an appointment for you to see Dr Forrest on Monday.'

She sat up, shaking the hair out of her eyes. 'It seemed best not to waste time,' I went on in a rush, 'but I didn't tell Daddy. He's been upset enough as it is and I don't want any more worries to interfere with his painting schedule.'

'What time on Monday?'

'Four-thirty.'

'After school?'

I hesitated. 'If you feel up to going to school.'

'Mother, I must! I missed three whole days this week. I've a lot to make up as it is.' She looked up at me. 'How much do they know, at school?'

'I'm not sure, but since there were quite extensive police enquiries going on, some of them must have guessed. Just say you had amnesia. That's the truth, anyway. It might well be just the strain of A-levels.'

'Coming events casting their shadows? I don't think so. I think the shadows over me come from events past. Is Roger coming tomorrow? He seemed to know what he was talking about. I think I'll have a word with him—on a strictly impersonal level, of course.'

'I think it would be better to wait till you see Dr Forrest. I'm quite sure he knows more than Roger.'

'I suppose so. Do you remember what he was saying about dual personality?'

'Not really. It was just as the lights went out. He never finished.'

'It sounds weird, doesn't it?'

'Very.' There seemed to be a tight band round my head against which my temples throbbed agonisingly. When had all this strangeness settled over us? Briony's headaches had only started a few months ago, but her accurate flashes of precognition dated back to her early childhood. Perhaps the course had been set even then. Where would it end?

Briony slept and the hot sun crept round the garden. I closed my eyes, drifting in a demi-world of shapes and fancies, refusing to let my mind alight on any one long enough to unmask it and see it for what it was. Colours and forms changed constantly against my eyelids as the sun and shadows stretched and moved. I wished it were possible to lie in this warm limbo indefinitely, without the ever-hovering necessity of returning to the real world and its unreal problems.

The click of the side gate roused me as it had last week to Edgar's arrival. This time it was Simon Pomfrett who came strolling over the grass. 'What a shockingly lazy scene!' he greeted us. 'Compared with you, our garden's a hive of industry. I've just finished cutting the grass and I even bribed Roger to go round the edges with the new clippers.'

'Good for you. Briony, get a chair for Mr Pomfrett, will you. In fact, bring three more. I'm going to put the kettle on now, and perhaps

Daddy and Mrs Pomfrett will join us.'

Lance seemed a little more relaxed as we all had tea together and I reflected that perhaps painting did help him to unwind as he claimed. He was obviously satisfied with the afternoon's work and that also eased his anxiety. Nevertheless, I noticed that he kept glancing across at Briony, repeatedly bringing her into the conversation, and her own attitude became increasingly wary. And suddenly, without warning, we were thrown once again into the whirlpool of doubt and uncertainty. It all started so innocuously. A large furry bee alighted on the sugar basin and started to make its way labouriously round the rim. As we watched it lost its balance and fell on to the glistening white pile, sending out a shower of grains as it struggled wildly to regain its footing. Briony, laughing, helped it to right itself with the handle of her teaspoon and it bumbled agitatedly away.

'That reminds me of the time a bee fell into the lemonade, and you said—' She broke off and frowned.

'—that if we only had some whisky handy, we'd have had instant toddy,' Lance finished.

She looked up at him quickly. 'Yes.'

Simon and Stella were smilingly unaware of the sudden tension, but I knew perfectly well that such an eposide had never happened to Briony. It was a memory in which she herself had played no part. Well, Max, I thought, what would you make of that? Can it be explained by freak telepathy, Briony somehow reading Lance's memory of that other time?

'Are you sure you can cope with us tomorrow?' Simon was saying. 'We'd rather written it off for this weekend.'

'We'd love to see you if you've nothing else arranged, and the children too. Cynthia and Edgar are coming, of course.'

'And the Forrests?' asked Stella.

'No,' Lance returned smoothly, 'not the Forrests this week.'

'I must admit I'm rather relieved. Paula's so elegant and sophisticated even in a swimsuit that she makes me feel blowsy and—overblown.'

'Especially when you haven't had your hair done!' put in Simon wickedly, with a wink at me.

'She said I should wear it short and wash it myself!' Stella said indignantly. 'I wouldn't have *her* hairstyle for a million pounds!'

Lance put his cup and saucer on the tray and stood up. 'If you'll all excuse me I must be getting back to work. Thanks again for coming this afternoon, Stella.'

'A pleasure. We must go too.'

Briony and I walked to the gate with the Pomfretts, then, announcing she had had enough sunbathing, she went into the house. I carried the tea tray back to the kitchen and put it on the table. The grains of sugar which the

140

bee spilt had melted in the heat into tiny transparent spots of stickiness. I stood for a long moment looking down at them. Where and when had that other episode with the bee taken place? Could it perhaps have been somewhere in Scotland in, say, nineteen fifty-eight?

CHAPTER NINE

Saturday's sunshine had not reappeared by the time that the first visitors arrived the next day, and for the adults at least the pool did not seem so inviting. Mark, Briony and the two young Pomfretts had a swim, but the sky remained grey and cloudy and they changed straight back into trews and sweaters. The rest of us—Stella and Simon, Cynthia and Edgar and Lance and I—sat on the terrace, talking intermittently. I knew Cynthia was full of questions about Briony's disappearance, but either Edgar had warned her not to raise the subject or some latent tact of her own kept her silent.

Lance, I noticed with faint surprise, was unusually smartly dressed. Normally he went about the house and garden in an old shirt and paint-spattered trousers, but today he wore a shirt I didn't remember seeing before and his trousers, narrow and sand-coloured, also

141

seemed new. A silk cravat was tucked casually into his neck. He seemed restless and unable to relax, particularly when Briony was out of sight, making excuses to go over and watch the swimming, and later standing at the net when the young people played tennis. Mark at least seemed ill at ease in his company and I was uncomfortably aware that a resentment was building up between the two of them, almost as though they were the same age and resented the other's interest in Briony.

The other undeniable awkwardness was between myself and Edgar. The erratic progress of our awareness of each other—one step forward and two back—did nothing to smooth the way for naturalness when we met in company. Distractedly I tried to remember exactly what had been said between us at our last meeting, but had only a rather unsettling memory of his arms round me and my hand in his. It would be very easy to lean on Edgar's dependability, even to accept his soothing comfort when things became fraught as they seemed increasingly to do, but I knew that only a very fine line separated such acceptances from something much deeper. For his part, after years of rebuff with Cynthia he was probably more than ready to turn to me, might even already imagine himself in love. All of this was a complication I hadn't time to consider with the attention it called for.

Over lunch the rift between Lance and Mark

widened embarrassingly. I can't remember how it started except that it was something to do with a disputed point in the tennis foursome. It seemed that Mark had smashed the ball into the back of the court, thereby losing the set, when a gentle tap, or so Lance insisted, would have dropped it just over the net and saved the day. The hypothetical argument became quite heated. Mark, a polite boy, had flushed and I could see was only with difficulty holding back a stronger retort than manners would allow. Whether a challenge was actually issued I don't know, but it was all at once clear that he and Lance were to embark on a singles game to establish who was the better player.

'What about handicaps?' Simon enquired, entering into the spirit of the thing. 'Mark must be a lot fitter than you, old boy.'

'Not at all,' Lance answered tightly. 'I play on and off at weekends and am in pretty good shape. I'm certainly not going to accept any kind of advantage. We'll play on a level footing and see who wins.'

'Okay, if you say so. I'll come and be umpire.'

'I'm not going to miss this!' Stella remarked, and so it was that we all made our way to the bottom of the garden and set up chairs alongside the court. To be fair, the opponents did seem to be evenly matched. They were much the same height and although Lance could give Mark twenty years, there was little difference in weight. I stole a glance at Briony, sitting with Lindsay and Roger on the grass at our feet, and noticed the excitement in her. I was not surprised. Those two were playing for her favours as surely as knights in a tournament five hundred years ago.

The game began. Lance played with flair and style, Mark more slowly but powerfully. At the net Simon, perched on a step ladder, kept meticulous score. For a while the points went to the server but at the end of the first set Lance broke through to win 8—6. Elated by this success, his play became noticeably more erratic. He was also, though he would never have admitted it, beginning to tire. Each point had to be fought for, sometimes with several deuces, and by the end of the second set, which Mark won, they had been playing for over an hour. Stella had discreetly fallen asleep behind her sunglasses but at my feet Briony, hugging her knees, intently watched every stroke. I wondered which of them she wanted to win. For myself I was tired of sitting in one position and uncomfortable at the less than sportsmanlike atmosphere of the game. As inconspicuously as possible I left the court and made my way aimlessly through the fruit trees to the walled kitchen garden which was old Jack's pride and joy.

'Mind if I join you?' Edgar had fallen into step behind me. I smiled vaguely in reply, and

144

after a moment he said quietly, 'Just what do you suppose he's trying to prove?'

I gave a little shrug. 'I don't know.'

'What's the matter, Ann?' His voice was gentle and almost my undoing, but how could I possibly begin to tell him?

'Nothing,' I lied. Up and down the narrow little paths we walked, past the straggling peas and scarlet runners, the netted preserves where strawberries were slowly ripening and alongside the wide neat rows of potatoes, onions and lettuces. I kept walking, guessing that if I stopped here in the seclusion of the walled garden Edgar's arms would come round me and I would not have the strength or the will to resist him. We completed the square in silence and came out again on to the lawn, closing the door in the wall behind us. A scattering of applause greeted a good shot—whose, we had no way of knowing.

Edgar said, 'What will happen if he loses?'

'I don't know. Somehow I don't think he will. He can't afford to.'

'I'm sorry for that boy,' he said abruptly. 'He doesn't deserve this.'

'I know.'

We stood in the middle of the lawn, unwilling to return to the court, unable to leave it completely. The garden stretched away towards the house, the deserted pool on the right, the rose garden and Lance's studio on the left.

'This is a fabulous place, isn't it?' Edgar remarked. 'The grounds are so attractive and the house itself pure Queen Anne.'

'Yes, I love it.'

'I remember when you and Lance bought it, and how you had all the old paint scraped away down to the original honey-coloured wood. The house seemed to come alive again, as though it had been waiting for you.' He gave an embarrassed laugh. 'Just as well Cynthia didn't hear that burst of rhetoric!'

'One of the advantages of being married to an artist is that he knows just the right colours to complement the woodwork and style of architecture.'

'Yes, that terracotta in the hall was a real brainwave. The sitting-room colour scheme's built round the painting, isn't it?'

I turned to stare at him, my instinctive denial melting away unspoken. Because he was right. The soft blues and greens of the furniture, the oatmeal carpet and the vivid cyclamen of the long curtains were all repeated in the canvas over the fire-place. It seemed unbelievable that I should have failed to realise it. The painting had dominated our lives even more than I'd appreciated.

'Funny, that outburst last weekend,' Edgar was going on, unaware of the disturbance his previous remark had caused me, 'with that analyst chap staring at the painting and Lance all on the defensive. I thought for a moment they were going to come to blows!'

146

I said rockily, 'We'd better go back and see how the game's progressing.'

Mark and Lance, faces flushed and shining with sweat, shirts sticking to their backs, were still playing hard. Stella had woken up and was chatting to Cynthia. Lindsay, apparently having lost interest, was lying back on the grass with her eyes closed, while her brother whittled at a twig with his penknife. Of them all, Briony was the only one who didn't seem to have moved during our absence as every fibre of her concentrated on the game in play.

As it happened, we arrived just in time to see the end. The score was eight all in the final set when Mark, stretching backwards to slam a ball, stumbled and twisted his ankle. It was obvious the game would have to be abandoned and although the ankle was swelling rapidly and seemed painful, I couldn't help being thankful that an honourable finish had been possible. Briony hovered anxiously as Mark limped back to the house between Edgar and Simon, with the young Pomfretts bringing up the rear. Lance watched them go with a frown.

'I shouldn't have thought he was hurt as badly as all that.'

'The wounded hero always gets the acclaim,' Cynthia remarked acidly. She linked her arm through his, giving it a squeeze. 'Never mind, my sweet. If they want to make a fuss of him, let them. *I* thought you played magnificently.'

'It would have been much more satisfactory

to have had a definite result,' he muttered. 'Damn the boy! I just about had him, too.'

'You'd better put your sweater on,' I said quietly. 'You're very hot and there's quite a cool breeze.' Seeing the hurt bafflement on his face, I added, 'And well played, darling. Cynthia's right, you were magnificent.'

Leaving him to her ministrations I quickened my steps to catch up with the others. 'Briony, find a stool to prop Mark's foot up while I organise a cold water compress. He'll have to rest it now.'

The afternoon slid away in an atmosphere of anti-climax. Briony was still in the grip of her new-found power, seeming deliberately to play Lance and Mark against each other as though to prolong the excitement of their contest. Lance's attention, though he kept well away from Mark, was centred entirely on her. I saw Edgar's frown as his eyes went from one of them to the other, and my heart sank. I was relieved when, at about six o'clock, the party began to break up. Simon offered to take Mark home, since he obviously couldn't ride his bicycle.

As he prepared to hobble into the car, the boy turned to us. 'Thank you for the super lunch, Mrs Tenby. And thanks for the game, sir. You certainly kept me on my toes!' The hopeful look he gave Lance was an obvious mixture of apology and conciliation, but Lance, to my regret, merely gave a curt nod and hoped formally that the swelling would

148

soon go down. I knew from Mark's face as he turned away that he realised his tentative olive branch had been rejected. It may well have been his downcast expression which led Briony to reach up quickly to kiss him. It was all innocent enough but the effect was disconcerting. While Mark flushed, smiled and got in the car, Lance turned on his heel and walked abruptly away.

'That was hardly tactful,' I chided her as the car drove off.

'Why?' She tossed back her hair and eyed me with unusual defiance.

'Because you knew Daddy was watching and was annoyed with Mark anyway.'

'So what?' she answered pertly. 'Hasn't it occurred to him that Mark and I occasionally do more than hold hands?'

'That will do!' I said sharply. She deflated suddenly and turned to watch Lance striding in the direction of the studio.

'Had I better go after him?'

'No!' I said quickly, and surprised myself by my vehemence. I added more reasonably, 'He'll have calmed down by supper time.'

But the tensions of the day were far from over. Briony went up to her room to do some revision and I tried to relax for a while with the Sunday papers, but my mind was too intent on my own problems to take in the world's. Eventually I laid them down and leant my head back, staring moodily up at *Eternal Spring*. Could this really be the source of all the trouble

149

brewing up about us? I had the illogical conviction that it was. By this time tomorrow, Briony would have seen Max. A little tremor of apprehension shivered over me. What would we know tomorrow that as yet we hardly dared to suspect?

I stood up quickly and went outside to lean on the balustrade. Belated sunshine was now gilding the heavy purple clouds and pouring its mellow spotlight on the leaves of the trees. Over by the vegetable garden two pigeons cooed to each other. I hoped they had not been eating the new peas. I walked slowly down the steps and along to the studio. Lance was painting feverishly, his back to me. In the foreground of the canvas sat a figure which was unmistakably Stella, her hair soft and loose, her breast swelling at the low neck of her blouse. Beyond, a cornfield stretched in a riot of colour which suggested evening sunshine as surely as its counterpart out in the garden. Here and there its deep gold was splashed with the vermilion blaze of poppies and in the distance lay indistinct humps of purple hills. The whole painting was vibrant with life, a startling contrast to his last completed canvas of a waterfall in muted greys and blues.

'Behold her single in the field",' I quoted softly, and he spun round.

'Hello, I didn't hear you come.' He paused. 'What do you think of it?'

'Very striking.'

He turned frowningly back to his painting. 'Did I make a fool of myself this afternoon?'

'It wasn't a particularly dignified performance.'

'That's what I feared. I don't know what got into me. That boy seemed so sure of himself, so *young*. Anyway, I felt he needed teaching a lesson. Whether it came off or not I don't know. If it's any comfort to him, I shall suffer for it tomorrow! I'm seizing up already.'

I started to massage his neck and shoulders, feeling some of the tension ease away. 'Can't you stop now? It's nearly supper time.'

'All right. I'll just clean the brushes.'

I turned away, my eyes falling on the untidy pile of sketches and pieces of paper littering the table. What made me lift the top one I'll never know, but immediately below it lay a sketch of the same face that Briony had drawn repeatedly and with such compulsion. Without a word Lance took the paper out of my hand and dropped it back in place, concealing the other. I turned slowly and met his eyes and for a long moment we looked at each other, he seeming to dare me to ask for an explanation, I not daring to. Then he said heavily, 'Let's go back to the house.'

Supper was a silent meal. As usual on a Sunday evening, Mrs Rose had laid out a selection of quiches and flans and we helped ourselves. I had the uneasy feeling that Briony was holding herself in check, that inside her a

151

tightly coiled spring threatened to fly apart.

After repeatedly failing in his attempts to catch her eye, Lance said abruptly, 'Have you forgiven me for this afternoon?'

'What about this afternoon?'

'The ill-judged game of tennis.'

'It was very good. I enjoyed it.'

'I'm glad someone did,' he replied bitterly, and was unable to stop himself adding, 'You'll probably have to dispense with your swain's company on the way home from school next week.'

Briony's chin came up. 'You were rather horrid to him.'

'He was rather horrid to me, but you didn't kiss me.'

She stared at him for a moment, a flush creeping over her skin. She looked young, disturbed and touchingly unsure of herself. I wanted to scream at them to stop hurting each other, but I could only sit listening to the uneven pounding of my heart.

Lance looked away first, and after a moment she went on eating in silence. I said in a rush, 'Daddy got on very well with the painting this afternoon' and then could have bitten my tongue out. Suppose she went along to see? Suppose she casually lifted a sketch as I had, to be confronted with her own 'self portrait', drawn this time by Lance?

But she merely replied without interest, 'Good,' and silence settled over us again. The

152

meal over, we returned to the sitting-room. The french windows were still open and the air felt chilly. Lance went over and closed them. Briony selected a magazine and dropped into an easy chair, one leg curled beneath her. I picked up the discarded paper and handed half of it to Lance.

For half an hour or so a kind of peace reigned. I read the film and theatre reviews and turned to the book page. I think it was the quality of Lance's silence rather than Briony's soft humming which finally penetrated my attention. She was still idly flicking through the magazine, apparently unaware of his riveted attention. Yet another crisis was about to be forced upon us, I realised wearily. Once again the role of peacemaker would presumably have to be mine. With a dull sense of inevitability I waited for the storm to break. Even so, when it came I jumped.

'What's that you're humming?' The question lashed across the room like a jet of steam. Briony laid down her magazine and looked at him in surprise and the gasp I gave seemed to rip my throat apart. For it was no longer Briony who sat there. The nameless thing I had been dreading had actually happened and I saw for myself the stranger who usurped my daughter's place.

Yet what difference was there? As Mark had said, it was hard to pinpoint. Obviously the physical features were the same, yet the

153

attitude, the whole aura was different. The face looked subtly older, more assured, and as I watched unbelievingly a slow smile spread over it, the smile a girl would give not to her father but to a lover, tender, teasing and provocative.

'You know quite well what I was humming,' she answered softly, and the faint Scottish intonation stabbed at my cringing eardrums. Lance was gazing at her as though mesmerised. He said in a hoarse whisper, 'Sing the words.'

Softly and indescribably sweetly, she did so:

"'And fare-thee-weel, my only Luve,
And fare-thee-weel, a while!
And I will come again, my Luve,
Tho' 'twere ten thousand mile!'"

I knew it, of course. It was the last verse of the lovely song by Robert Burns, 'My Luve is like a red, red rose.' But in the hush of that listening room, with the picture on the wall seeming to pulsate with a life of its own, it came across the years as a clear promise. 'I will come again, my Luve—'

With a muffled sound Lance bowed his head into his hands. I sat unmoving, my straining eyes on the girl's face. And as I watched, the consciously provoking smile faded and a tremor shook the image like a pebble shivering the reflection in a pond. A faintly puzzled expression emerged, followed quickly by fear. Across Lance's bent head, Briony's own

154

questioning eyes met mine as her lips framed the words, 'What happened?'

I shook my head helplessly. She said aloud, alarm in her voice, 'Daddy?'

Slowly he raised his white, haunted face to stare at her.

'What is it, Daddy? Are you ill? Will someone please tell me what's the matter?' Her voice began to rise.

'Nothing,' I said at last, from a great distance. 'It's all right, darling, Daddy's only tired. The tennis wore him out more than he'll admit.'

Lance made a supreme effort and smiled. 'Yes, I'm only tired,' he repeated mechanically. My heart ached for him. I knew he doubted the reality of what he had seen, but how could I reassure him, at Briony's expense?

After a moment, as her eyes flickered from his face back to me, she said, 'I'm tired, too. I think I'll go to bed.' She stood up, hesitated, then came to kiss us each in turn. Lance sat like a statue. I said, 'Good-night, dear, sleep well.'

The door closed behind her. As though released from a spell, Lance stood up and lumbered blindly towards the french windows.

'No!' I said ringingly. He stopped and turned in surprise. 'You always run away, don't you?' My voice shook dangerously. 'At the first sign of something wrong, you make for the studio like a wounded animal for its lair. Doesn't it ever occur to you that I haven't any

155

sanctuary other than you?'

He stood staring down at me and I could see him struggling to free himself from the strands of the nightmare he had just lived through in order to take in what I was saying.

I stood up. 'Lance, I need you. Please don't go.' The tortured incomprehension in his eyes was almost more than I could bear. I said more gently, 'Darling, you weren't dreaming and you're not insane. I saw it too.' He was still standing in the middle of the room and I went over to him and put my arms tightly round him. I might have been holding a block of stone. 'Whatever it seemed like, she's ill. That's all it is. There are times when she doesn't know what she's doing. It won't help if we panic. We must just try to stay calm and help her all we can. Darling, don't look like that!' My voice shook again. I reached up and kissed him on the mouth. His skin felt cold and clammy. There was no response. 'Sit down and I'll pour you a drink.'

I went to the cabinet and took out two glasses, listening intently for the sounds of movement which would tell me he was responding more normally. To my untold relief I heard him stumble back to his chair. When I handed him the glass of brandy he was almost composed apart from his pallor. His eyes met mine gravely.

'I'm sorry, Ann. You're quite right, I'm a selfish devil.'

156

'I didn't say that,' I protested gently.

'But it's true. As you said, I run away and leave you at the first hint of trouble. I must have let you down countless times over the years. It's a wonder you've stayed with me.'

'Oh now look, there's no need to go on like that! All I meant—'

'I know what you meant, but all the same it's been a pretty one-sided affair, this marriage, hasn't it? I wonder how many times you've regretted agreeing to it.'

'Lance, please! I've *never* regretted it. I—'

He said unsteadily, 'I had the best of intentions, you know. I only wanted to look after you and—and Briony. I thought it would work.'

'And hasn't it?' My whispered challenge seemed to echo round the room. He took a sip of his drink, his eyes never leaving mine. Then he said quietly, 'You tell me.'

And at that moment, probably the most important we had faced in sixteen years, the telephone began to ring. I was incapable of moving. Lance went to answer it. I heard the tone of his voice change, become incredulous and animated. I didn't hear what he was saying. I don't think if I'd been standing right next to him that I would have heard. The conversation seemed to go on a long time. 'I thought it would work,' he'd said. And, 'You tell me.' And beneath the surface of that hurt was the terrifying strangeness in Briony.

157

'Ann!' He had come back at last, an excited smile on his face. 'You'll never guess who that was! Do you remember hearing me speak of Gordon MacIntyre? We exchange Christmas cards every year. He was my great friend at art school—a wonderful character. I haven't seen him for twenty years! He was phoning to say he has to be in London for a couple of days next week and could we meet. I told him he must stay here, with us.'

He had completely forgotten what we'd been talking about when the phone rang. Seemingly unaware of my silence, he added enthusiastically, 'You'll like Gordon. Lord, I can hardly believe it! Old Gordon, after all these years!'

In his excitement he didn't seem to register, as I had immediately done, that yet another piece of the past, of that threatening, unknown world of the art school, was about to encroach on our beleaguered present. But I realised it, and the knowledge brought nothing more positive than an anaesthetised acceptance.

CHAPTER TEN

The next morning, though I would have liked to stop them both, Lance went to college and Briony to school. At breakfast there had been a new wariness between them. Lance was again

158

dressed in what I assumed were new clothes, this time an electric blue denim suit, a soft shirt and wide floppy tie. He looked smart but somehow slightly off-key, as though the style were rather too young for him. Some comment seemed called for, so I remarked lightly, 'You're looking very trendy again. When did you splash out on this new wardrobe?'

'Last week. Do you like it?' The question was addressed to Briony.

She nodded without much interest. 'Mark has one rather similar.'

Lance flushed but all he said was, 'I presume you want a lift?'

'If you don't mind.' I noticed she had hardly eaten anything.

'I'll get the car out. See you later, Ann.'

'I might not be in when you get back,' I said quickly, and at his look of enquiry, added rather less than truthfully, 'Briony has to see the doctor again this evening.' When he had gone out, I added, 'I'll pick you up as near school as I can park. And please darling take things gently. Don't be in too much of a hurry to catch up on what you missed.'

She smiled briefly and was gone. I poured myself another cup of coffee and tried to forget the appointment which hung over us. At nine o'clock Moira Cassidy tapped on the door and put her head round. 'I'm so glad Briony's home safely. Did you find out what happened?'

'Not really, no. She has no recollection of the

journey to Scotland.'

'It's a little frightening, isn't it?'

'It is, rather.'

She hesitated but when I didn't enlarge on my agreement she smiled and withdrew.

A little later I phoned Jan Staveley to enquire after Mark's ankle. Most of the swelling had gone down and she thought he'd be back at school the next day. 'How's Briony?' she asked.

'So-so.' I didn't want to go into details. Certainly I had no intention of telling anyone I was taking her to see Max Forrest.

'I presume the disappearance was just an extension of what I told you about?'

'I imagine so. I'm trying not to worry about it. Dr Burton's seen her again. It's probably overwork as much as anything.'

'You'll be glad when the exams are over.'

I knew I'd implied that overwork had been the doctor's diagnosis and that Jan had accepted my remark at face value. It was just another of the half-truths with which my life suddenly seemed peppered.

As the day passed, the muscles in my stomach tightened apprehensively. Would Max be able to help us? And what form would such help take? The implications of psychiatry raised bogeys I wasn't equipped to face, riddled with superstitious horror tales of mediaevel Bedlam. Please not hospitalisation, I thought frantically—not for Briony.

My anxiety and general restlessness propelled me out of the house to meet her long before the necessary time and I was forced to park the car in the full heat of the afternoon sun. Even with all the windows open I was hot and uncomfortable and the waiting time seemed interminable, yet when at last she opened the car door and slid in beside me I would willingly have waited endless hours more. Now, no delay was possible. It was time to go. I switched on the engine and pulled away from the curb.

The Suffolk countryside had never looked lovelier. It impinged on my attention beyond the pulse which fluttered at the base of my throat and the concentration I tried to keep anchored on my driving. We splashed through a ford and climbed the slope on the other side. Hens squawked agitatedly, running in an ungainly manner from the car's approach, and a few ducks hunched by the roadside in neckruffs of emerald feathers.

Bury St Edmunds, said a road sign. I had always loved Bury, with its living tapestry of history, the Norman buildings and the Inns where pilgrims had rested on their way to St Edmund's shrine. The very street names evoked the richness of its memories—Cornhill, Butter Market, Looms Lane, and, on a more ecclesiastical note, Abbey Gate and Abbot's Bridge. Today, however, it was merely the outer strands of the web which waited to entrap us.

I stopped the car outside a tall stone house in a street of tall stone houses, each with whitened steps leading to the front door and an array of brass plates shining in the sunlight.

'Well,' I said unnecessarily, 'here we are.'

We were shown into the waiting-room, well appointed with comfortable sofas and chairs, a coffee table laden with magazines and a window looking out down the long narrow garden. Almost immediately a pleasant, quiet-voiced woman came to collect us.

'Mrs Tenby? Will you both come this way, please?'

Max Forrest was at the door of his room to meet us. In his clerical grey suit and snowy shirt he looked entirely different from the informal little man whose hirsute body had so disgusted Cynthia. Numbly I sat where he indicated, Briony on my left, and Max resumed his chair behind the handsome mahogany desk.

'Now, Briony,' he began pleasantly, 'I want you to tell me as fully as possible what's been worrying you. Take your time and think carefully, mentioning anything, however unimportant it may seem to you, which might have a bearing on your illness.'

I saw her eyes widen at the word 'illness'. Obviously she had not considered that aspect, but I was surprised at how concisely she listed for him the various instances of strangeness. It was clear she had given it all a lot of thought.

She even referred back to the childhood flashes of clairvoyance which I had hoped she'd forgotten. The headaches, she said, had started about six months ago and become progressively worse. The first time she was aware of having lost consciousness was when I found her on the rug the previous week, but there had been times which were less than clear in her mind when, as she put it, she felt as though she were sleepwalking but knew she wasn't. It seemed likely that these were the occasions Mark had noticed. She hesitated fractionally when she came to the faces she had drawn and labelled 'self portrait', but the first real sign of agitation came as she spoke of finding herself in Scotland with no recollection of how she'd arrived there.

'And I think,' she finished, 'that I passed out for a moment or two last night, though Mother and Daddy didn't actually say so.'

Max looked across at me with raised eyebrows and I nodded slightly. I was glad that Briony's own recollections had spared me from having to disclose Mark's confidence.

Max had been making notes all this time, as had the pleasant-faced woman who sat inconspicuously in a corner of the room. I noticed that she had a cassette recorder on her desk.

'Thank you,' Max said as Briony stopped speaking. 'That is all very clear and a great help to me. Now, is there anything else at all you can

163

think of? Any especially vivid or recurring dreams, perhaps?'

To my surprise she flushed, glanced at me and away again. 'There have been, yes, but I'd rather not talk about them.'

'Very well,' Max said smoothly, 'we'll leave that for the moment. So that's about all you can remember. I asked your mother to come in with you initially so that I could explain to both of you how we intend to set about making you better. If there's anything you don't understand, I hope that you will ask me to explain in greater detail.

'First of all, we will start with a series of rather boring tests—I.Q., behaviour, association and so on. Then, if you are agreeable, it would probably be very helpful to try by means of hypnosis to discover the root of the trouble. That is our only way of probing the unconscious, where so much that is blocked to the waking mind can be causing disturbance.' He paused. 'You are quite happy about hypnosis? You will trust me?'

Her eyes were fixed on his face. 'Yes.' I felt she was half hynotised already.

'That is very good. So often complete analysis and therefore a cure is delayed because a patient resists hypnosis, but of course there is absolutely nothing to worry about. You simply relax, and I usually end by initiating a period of normal sleep so that when you wake you will feel completely rested. You're looking tired, my dear. Have you not been sleeping very well?'

Again the guilty flush. 'Not very.'

'The dreams you spoke of have been disturbing you?'

'Yes.'

Max rose to his feet. 'Very well, Mrs Tenby. I hope you have some idea now of the way we will be working, and if you will wait in the other room Briony and I will start straight away. My assistant will remain here throughout the treatment, making notes and occasionally using the recorder. At the end of the session I shall come through and have a word with you.'

The waiting-room. I remember every detail of it, every swirl of pattern on the carpet. Above the mantelpiece a tank of brightly coloured tropical fish swam ceaselessly, dipping and turning with fluid grace. I watched them for a long time. Through the open window came the normal, every-day sounds of another world. A smiling girl brought me a cup of tea. There was no clock in the room, but my eyes kept returning to the seemingly unmoving hands of my watch.

It was about an hour later that Max came. He seemed tired and drained, as though a large proportion of his energy had been transferred to Briony in her trance.

I stood up. 'Well?'

'Sit down, Ann.' I wondered if he realised he had used my first name. There was of course no

165

reason why he should not. He lowered himself wearily on to the sofa, his dark skin contrasting strongly with its creamy chintz. There was an abstracted look in his eyes, as though his mind had not yet fully relinquished its absorbing study of Briony's.

'Did you find out anything?' I blurted in an agony of impatience.

'Indeed yes. She was a perfect subject for hypnosis, needing only the slightest suggestion for everything to come pouring out.'

'And—what did?' My lips were so dry that they kept sticking together and I had to force them apart to speak, making an odd little popping sound.

He said slowly, 'I must confess to you that this is one of the most fascinating cases I've come across. Quite incredible. It emerged clearly under hypnosis that there are two distinct personalities present. I had suspected as much.'

'Dual personality?' I whispered.

His black eyes darted to my face. 'Yes. I mentioned it that day at your home, did I not? It is a very strange phenomenon but we are coming to believe it is far more widespread than we had realised. It could account for quite a lot of the amnesia cases we come across. However, in Briony's case it is somewhat different.'

'How do you mean?' I asked fearfully.

'One of the common factors in such cases is

166

some trauma, usually in childhod, which triggers off the dissociation. Yet although Briony was so relaxed I was completely unable to find any such distress. In fact she seems a particularly happy child, well loved and secure. Believe me, this is most unusual.'

'There's something else, isn't there? Something else unusual?'

He smiled slightly. 'You're very perceptive, Ann. Yes, there is something else and I have to confess I am at a loss to know how to account for it. As is usual during therapy I had regressed with her, led her back stage by stage over the years in the search for this trauma. I had found nothing and was considering regressing still further—some psychiatrists have established proof of consciousness even before birth, in the uterus—when, without any warning, she was suddenly fully adult. I was, I must admit, completely taken aback, but before I could question her she cried out in a ringing voice, "I don't want to die!"'

I stared fixedly at his face, trying to read in it what he was going to say before he said it.

'And now we come to the difficult part. I can offer no explanation at this point, only tell you what occurred.' I nodded, unable to speak. 'There was obviously a grown woman present, and I could not see how we had reached her. So I asked her name. She said it was Ailsa Cameron. Does the name mean anything to you?'

167

'Nothing at all.'

'This is very important, because it's the first instance of deviation. Throughout the regression I kept asking her name and her age at each of the stages. Each time she had presented herself as Briony Tenby. I presume she took your second husband's name on your marriage?'

'Yes.' The drumming in my head remained consistent.

'She told me that she was twenty years old and lived in a Scottish village called Drumlochhead.'

He waited for my reaction. I could only dumbly shake my head.

'She mentioned that she was in love with a man called Jamie and that they both attended Glasgow School of Art. And there was something about a particular painting, but it was all so confused at that point that I couldn't unravel it. Perhaps when I replay the cassette—Now, it was, of course, to Scotland that Briony went last week.'

'Yes.'

'Has she ever shown any desire to go before?'

'Never. Quite the reverse.' I tried to collect myself. 'I met Lance in Scotland when she was a baby. I'd always assumed that was the reason for her obsession with everything Scottish.'

'But I thought you said—'

'That she didn't want to go there? That's true, and it surprised me very much. I thought she'd be delighted but she became almost hysterical when I suggested it. She kept saying something about it's not being time.'

'Yet in her fugue she made her way straight there. Fascinating. And in that state she even assumed a Scottish identity.'

'She? But you said there were two personalities?'

'That is so, but although there is a plurality of systems, the normal waking self is Briony.'

I stared at him uncomprehendingly. 'Then why should she assume another name?'

'That is the usual form in such cases, to differentiate between the personalities. The only interesting point is that she should choose a different nationality from her own. I wondered whether perhaps she recollected the name from some story book she'd read as a child, where perhaps the hero and heroine were Jamie and Ailsa.'

I said aridly, 'I've never heard of an Ailsa, but Briony's boy-friend told me she sometimes calls him Jamie.'

'Ah! So there is a positive link.'

'Max.' I leant forward, my fingers interlinked tightly. 'Lance has heard of Jamie, too.'

'Lance has?'

'Yes. I asked him if he'd ever known anyone of that name and he said—he said he had once, in another existence.'

'Another existence?' Max repeated softly.

169

'What a curious phrase to use.'

I made myself go on. 'This Ailsa said she'd been to Glasgow School of Art?'

'Yes.'

'Lance was there too.'

'But that is excellent! Your daughter's dream identity is strongly related to your husband, of whom we know she is very fond. Perhaps he mentioned this Jamie in her hearing once, and she knows he was at the art school. It could be an attempt to be closer to him which caused the deviation.'

'Those dreams she referred to,' I said with difficulty. 'They were about Lance, weren't they?'

'They were.'

I couldn't ask any more about them. In any case I doubt if he would have told me. Dully I remembered Jan's amateur suggestion that Briony might have resented Lance and myself coming together. If Max were beginning to think along the same lines, it was important that he should know the true position.

Before I lost my courage, I said, 'You say Briony could be making an unconscious attempt to be closer to Lance. I think you should know that actually she's always been closer to him than I have myself.'

'Indeed?' The word was polite, non-committal and impersonal, and I was grateful. Max was too good a psychologist to show sympathy; I would simply have broken down.

As it was, I was able to continue hesitantly.

'It was Briony who attracted him, when we first met. She was about eighteen months old and he—he was just infatuated with her. He was quite frank about it. He had had an unhappy love affair—I don't know any of the details—and hadn't intended to marry, but he couldn't let Briony go.'

'Are you not perhaps rather underestimating—?'

'No.' I shook my head emphatically. It was essential for Max to have the facts right. The salvaging of my pride was a consideration I couldn't afford.

'And you know nothing of this girl he once loved?'

'Nothing at all. I assumed she was with him at Art School, but I don't think he ever actually said so. Max, you did say all this has been known before, the splitting, and assuming a different name, and everything?'

'Yes, indeed. It is well documented in medical case histories.'

'Then why did you say Briony's case was especially interesting?'

'Well, although I had read of such cases, I had never observed one at first hand. Then, I was considerably surprised that Briony's own personality showed no abnormal restraint, which is usual when a feared, unpleasant side of the nature has been split off into a separate system. And thirdly, I am at a loss to

171

understand how I arrived at the dormant personality. This should either have emerged spontaneously or under hypnosis, in which case it would have appeared during regression at the age at which Briony had felt the need to dissociate. Yet all the way back through her childhood she insisted she was Briony Tenby.'

'So if there had been a split, it must have occurred even earlier?'

'It would seem so, but psychologically speaking that is impossible. An infant consciousness would have been incapable of taking refuge in a fully adult personality.'

The idea growing in my mind was also no doubt 'psychologically impossible.' But I was remembering the effect on Lance of Briony's abrupt transformation, especially her singing of the Burns song. I said carefully, 'An adult personality was present before Briony's babyhood?'

He shrugged, lifting his hands in an essentially foreign gesture. I was unable to put my grotesque idea into words and retreated into another more circuitous approach. 'Max—just suppose we find that someone called Ailsa Cameron actually existed?'

'It is a possibility. Some paranoids, for instance, call themselves Napoleon or Hitler.'

'But—suppose she was at art school with Lance? *Suppose she was the girl Lance once loved?*'

His eyes met mine in sudden, startled

172

understanding. But he merely replied after a moment, 'If your husband once spoke of her, it is possible—'

'But if he *didn't* speak of her?' I persisted doggedly. 'What then?'

'Even so it might be feasible for a strong mind like your husband's to impinge unknowingly on an unformed one such as Briony's.'

'Telepathy, you mean?'

'I am just saying it is a remote possibility.'

'But there is another one, isn't there?' I sat back, feeling my body trembling, the slippery sweat between the palms of my hands. Max made no reply, his eyes still intently on mine. 'A possibility,' I went on, 'which is probably no more remote and which actually fits all the facts more closely.' *I will come again, my luve—*

His eyes were still burning into mine. I moistened my lips.

'Might it not also be—feasible—for the girl who was Ailsa Cameron to have come back to Lance as my daughter?'

He had known, of course, what I was leading up to and made no comment on the enormity of my suggestion. He said, 'But she loved someone called Jamie. That was presumably how your husband lost her. We have no evidence that she died.'

That was true. Could I take it as a reprieve? The whole idea was so horrible, so devastating in its implications that I could hardly bear to

173

contemplate it. Yet Roger had said it was a widely held belief.

Max said gently, 'Ann, I am a psychiatrist. The word means "Healer of the soul." To heal something I must obviously first believe in it, but I do not necessarily believe in its transmigration from one existence to another. However, many great men do, psychiatrists among them. In the meantime I intend to continue to treat your daughter as a victim of hysterical dissociation. On that basis, if we can regain contact with the alternating consciousness of Ailsa, I shall repeat the behaviour and association tests I gave Briony. Perhaps then we may judge, from the extent of disparity in reactions just how wide the divergence between them is.'

'She'll have to come here again, then?' Stupidly, I had seen this visit as a once and for all solution to the problem.

'Indeed yes. Sometimes these cases can take years to disentangle.'

'Years!'

'I am not suggesting, of course, that it will be so long in this case. Briony is extremely co-operative and that is a great advantage.'

I said hesitantly, 'I might as well admit that Lance doesn't know I've brought her to see you. He was very much against the idea.'

'I had the impression that Lance himself was under a considerable strain. I suppose there's no possibility of persuading him to submit to treatment as well?'

'I shouldn't think so, no.' Shakily I opened my handbag and took out my powder compact to repair the ravages of the last half hour.

'I'm afraid this afternoon has not been easy for you, Ann. It may be some consolation to know that your frankness has been very helpful to me. And now I mustn't keep you any longer. I have suggested to Briony that she keeps a diary and makes detailed notes of any experience she undergoes. Perhaps she could bring it with her every time she comes. How about Thursday afternoon at the same time? Would that be convenient? And if at any time you need to contact me urgently out of office hours, the number is Rushyford 29. Briony should be waking up now. She won't remember anything that happened under hypnosis and I feel it would be unwise to refer to it for the moment.'

'Of course. Max—'

'Yes?'

'If—if it is possible for it to be— reincarnation, does that mean Briony never existed as herself?'

'No, no. I tell you there are *two* distinct personalities. If she were only this Ailsa there would be no disparity.'

'No, I suppose not.' It was all the comfort I had.

When Briony rejoined us she seemed calm and rested. 'Well, how did I do?' she asked Max with a little smile.

'Very well indeed. We'll soon have you sorted out.'

'It's an odd feeling, knowing I've been speaking to you but not what I've been saying. Almost like what's happened before.'

'But to much better effect, I assure you. I explained to your mother that regular attendance will be necessary until you're completely well again. I suggest you come back on Thursday afternoon, and don't forget to bring your diary with you.'

In the car going home, Briony said suddenly, 'I do wish Daddy wouldn't wear those "mod" clothes.'

I dragged my mind back from Max's observations and my own fears. 'I thought they were rather smart.'

'They make him look so young.'

'That might be the idea!'

'Well, I don't like it.' Her voice was sharp.

I said casually, 'Perhaps if you don't take any notice he'll stop bothering with them.'

'If *I* don't? You think he wears them to please me?'

'Possibly.' It was dangerous ground and I didn't know how to avoid it.

She said slowly, 'He's very attractive, isn't he? All the girls at school swoon about him. What was my real father like? Was he attractive, too?'

The car swerved slightly under my twitching

hands. It was many years since Briony had enquired after Michael. 'Yes, I suppose he was. I thought so, anyway.'

'Do I look like him?'

'A little.'

She lapsed back into silence and I was thankful. It was after six-thirty when we finally reached home and Lance was prowling up and down the sitting-room waiting for us.

'You were a long time,' he said accusingly.

'Yes, I'm sorry dear. I'll tell you about it after dinner. Have you had a good day?'

His eyes were on Briony and I sensed his discomfort. 'It was all right. How was school?'

'All right, too.'

After the meal Briony went upstairs to study and I watched her go with a guilty sense of relief. I handed Lance a cup of coffee and said lightly, 'Darling, I have a confession to make. It wasn't Dr Burton we went to see this evening; it was Max Forrest.'

Tensely I waited for his reaction. There was a long silence, then he said flatly, 'I can't say I'm surprised.'

'You don't mind?'

'It's a bit late to ask me that, isn't it?'

'I'm sorry, Lance. I know you didn't much care for him, but he's the only psychiatrist we know and I felt the matter was urgent.'

'So you decided to present me with a *fait accompli*.'

'Yes.' He made me feel ashamed.

177

'I'm not sure why you should imagine I'd object to anything that was for Briony's good.'

I said awkwardly, 'You did rather over-react last time I mentioned the matter.'

'Perhaps. But after—last night we obviously can't afford to mess around.'

'That's what I thought.'

'Though presumably you had already made the appointment?'

'Yes,' I admitted, 'as soon as we got back from Scotland.'

'And you thought I'd try to stop you taking her? She's your daughter, after all.' For the first time, his usual insistence on the lack of blood relationship between himself and Briony made some horrible kind of sense. 'Anyway, what was the verdict?'

'That it may well be a long job. He put her under hypnosis. I wasn't with her, of course.'

He was watching me intently. 'Did he tell you what happened?'

'A bit. It was all very medical and involved. I couldn't really understand. He seemed to regard this amnesia as a method of "opting out" but it puzzled him because Briony seemed so normal and happy that he couldn't see the reason for it.'

'It all sounds rather a waste of time, then.'

'I don't know. She seemed more relaxed afterwards.'

'Suppose this "opted out" existence is the one she chooses?'

I stared at him. 'It couldn't be.'

'Why couldn't it?'

'Well, she—she wouldn't be normal if it were.'

He said, 'I hope to Heaven she doesn't play up while Gordon's here.'

Gordon! I'd forgotten all about him. 'What time is he arriving?'

'He's travelling to London on the sleeper tonight. He'll go straight to his meetings and come on here tomorrow evening. He said he'd ring me from Liverpool Street to let me know which train to meet.'

'He'll just be here for one night?'

'Yes, he'll travel home from London on Wednesday. When is Briony due to see Forrest again?'

'Thursday evening, after school.'

'He didn't suggest we should keep her at home?'

'No. Presumably if it's to be a fairly long treatment, life has to carry on as much like normal as possible.'

'After last week, I'll be wondering every day if she's going to come home again.'

I pushed aside all the loathsome ambiguity in my mind, assuring myself that his reaction had been that of any father faced with his daughter's illness. Yet that night, as I lay awake in the dark, the treacherous doubts returned to plague me. Did he really *want* her to get better? Or would he be happier if her

179

alter ego was indeed the one she chose? What would happen if Ailsa Cameron, whoever she was or might have been, came to us permanently in Briony's place? Would Lance perhaps welcome her wholeheartedly, and if so would there be any room left in his life for me?

CHAPTER ELEVEN

By the next morning I had, of course, thought of lots of points I wished I'd mentioned to Max. For one thing, I had completely forgotten to tell him of my conviction that the painting had some kind of hold over Briony. He himself had been disturbed by it, so perhaps he wouldn't consider the idea too far-fetched. I firmly closed my mind to the other half of that memory—his difficulty in believing that Lance had painted it.

Briony went off to school, apparently happy enough. Lance retired as usual to the studio and Stella arrived for her sitting. Life seemingly went on, over and around the trials and obstacles of our existence. I checked that Mrs Rose was airing the guest-room bed for Gordon MacIntyre and arranged a small bowl of flowers on the dressing-table to add freshness and welcome. I gave explicit instructions for the evening meal and had a word with Dick Gifford about the herb bed.

And all the time, as Briony would have said, I felt that I was sleep-walking, playing a part, while my mind, untouched by all that was happening, continued in its real existence on a completely different plane.

At the end of her sitting, Stella joined me again for a cup of coffee. 'Lance is a bit up-tight these days, isn't he?' she commented, her large, china-blue eyes innocent over the rim of her cup.

'I'm afraid he is. He's worried about the rapidly dwindling time left to complete the quota of paintings, and of course this business about Briony gave him a shock.'

'Well, he's entitled to his artistic temperament. They say genius is next to madness. Look at Van Gogh!'

'He's hardly mad, Stella,' I said mildly.

'Sorry—how tactless can one be! It was meant as a back-handed compliment, meaning that he probably *is* a genius.' Her eyes went to *Eternal Spring*. 'Just look at that! It's positively brimming over with atmosphere.' But had Lance painted it? As my mind registered the subliminal question I was appalled at the perfidy of it. After all, his whole reputation stemmed from that painting. Yet I knew Max Forrest didn't believe that he was the artist. My faith in Max's judgment, so essential to my peace of mind over Briony's recovery, pulled me in half with regard to Lance.

'I presume you're coming to the W.I. this afternoon?'

'Sorry, what did you say?'

'The Women's Institute. Someone speaking on second marriages, I think.'

'Is it today? I'd forgotten all about it.'

'Do come. After all, you're quite an authority on the subject!'

'The trouble is that we're expecting a friend of Lance's this evening and I'm not sure what time he's arriving. We're waiting for a phone call.'

'We usually finish by about five anyway.'

It would certainly fill in the afternoon for me. Never had I been so conscious of the amount of time requiring to be 'filled in' until this last fortnight. Never before, perhaps, had I been so reluctant to be left alone with my thoughts.

'All right, Stella, I'll come. Two o'clock at the church hall.'

Gordon telephoned at lunch time. He was catching an earlier train than we'd anticipated, but Lance wouldn't hear of my cancelling the arrangement with Stella. 'A few minutes won't make any difference. No doubt we'll have plenty to talk about after all these years!'

Pale yesterday, he was now almost feverish with excitement. I looked at him with a sinking heart, unable to believe that yet another association with the past would, at the present time, be anything other than disastrous. Had

Gordon MacIntyre also known Jamie 'in another existence'? It seemed very likely.

The church hall that afternoon was a hive of gossiping, laughing women. Stella had kept me a seat between herself and Cynthia. Jan Staveley was two rows in front and Paula Forrest at the back with a woman I didn't know. I wondered briefly if Max had mentioned our visit but decided that it was unlikely. In any case, she merely raised her hand and smiled in greeting.

Notices were given out and minutes of the last meeting read. Had it really been only a month ago? I remembered almost with nostalgia the slides we had been shown of Israel. How unsuspecting I had been then of the troubles that lay ahead!

Maud Whittaker was taking the chair on this occasion and I tried hard to concentrate on what she was saying. 'We're very fortunate to have with us Mrs Leslie Tavistock, better known to us all, I'm sure, by her stage name of Penelope Styles. She's going to talk to us on the thorny subject of second marriages, with particular emphasis on those in the entertainment world. So, ladies, may I ask you to welcome Penelope Styles.'

We all clapped dutifully. I reflected with some acidity that our speaker had possibly mistaken our humble platform for a proper stage. Certainly her make-up, exquisite as it was, would have been more suitable behind the

183

footlights than in a church hall on a summer afternoon. I listened imperturbably to her opening remarks, unfairly prepared to be critical of any ideas she might have on marriage or anything else. As Maud had indicated, the talk was mainly slanted from the theatrical angle and could therefore have had little relevance for the worthy matrons who formed her audience. However, they were patently enthralled.

'For instance, it can be more than a little disconcerting,' Miss Styles gushed, 'to find that your brand new husband is required in his latest play to make passionate love to a beautiful woman possibly several years your junior!'

'Personally,' murmured Cynthia's sardonic voice in my ear, 'it would be a relief to know Edgar was capable of it!' I smiled obediently but my heart gave its usual painful little tug.

'And of course,' our speaker was continuing, 'it works both ways. It's hard to remain aloof towards an attractive man who clasps you in his arms twice nightly for a run of three months or so! Another problem, of course, is children. Many a second marriage has come unstuck because of a child's hostility to a new husband, while he on the other hand is very often jealous of the child.'

'That's never been one of your problems, has it darling?' came Cynthia's honied tones. 'Quite the reverse, in fact!'

My hands tightened on my bag but I made no reply. Quite the reverse. Did she mean that in my position she would be jealous of Briony? *Was* I, in some horrible perverted way, jealous of my husband's love for my daughter? Always before I had been able to brush the thought away as preposterous. Now, with the terrifying implications of the dormant Ailsa Cameron, things were no longer so clear cut.

I had lost the thread of the talk and didn't bother to pick it up again. My own worries crowded to the forefront of my mind, jostling for position until it seemed my head would burst. Lance and Briony. Lance and Briony. When I am dead and opened, I thought morbidly, paraphrasing Mary Tudor, you will find Lance and Briony lying in my heart.

Question time, and relatively little connection with the actual talk. The questions were mostly eager enquiries as to which of a host of well-known names Miss Styles knew personally. Only half listening, I was left with the impression that she knew them all. I found I was watching the time again, a habit with me these days. Would Briony be safely home from school yet? Had Gordon MacIntyre arrived?

The meeting broke up, I made my excuses and hurried to the car. I should have left a little earlier; the roads were clogged now with homeward-bound traffic. Fretting and fuming I was imprisoned behind a huge farm tractor and in the twisting lanes there was no hope of

185

overtaking. When eventually I turned in the gateway of the Lodge I saw Lance's car at the door. He must already have collected Gordon.

I hurried into the house and, guided by voices, out on to the terrace. Gordon MacIntyre turned at my approach, smiling and holding out his hand. As Lance had predicted, I liked him at once. He was tall and broad, a heavily made man with craggy features, thick sandy hair and steady grey eyes. His huge hand enveloped mine like a friendly paw as he cut short my apologies for not being home when he arrived.

'Gordon's brought a positive wealth of Scottish goodies,' Lance said with a smile. 'Shortbread, oatcakes—not to mention a magnificent bottle of whisky!'

'Not at all,' he replied in response to my thanks, 'I only hope my coming hasn't been too much of an inconvenience, but old Lance here wouldn't take no for an answer.' He threw him an affectionate glance. 'It's a bonny place you have here.'

'Yes, we're very fond of it.' Alarm bells clanged suddenly in my head as I looked around. 'Where's Briony?' I said quickly. 'She—'

'It's all right,' Lance broke in, 'she phoned Mrs Rose to say she'd be a little late. She was going back to the Pomfretts' to borrow something from Lindsay.'

'Oh.' I forced my heartbeats to slow down

186

and turned back to our guest. 'As a matter of fact, I don't think she knows you're coming. She was in bed when you phoned on Sunday and things were so chaotic yesterday I didn't get round to mentioning it.'

'Let's hope she survives the shock!' he said with a grin, and though I smiled, I silently echoed his words with deadly seriousness.

'Have you a family, Mr MacIntyre?'

'Gordon, please! Aye, I've two sons and a daughter. The elder boy is eighteen, just a little older than your lassie, I gather, and the other two slightly younger.'

Half my attention was straining for the sounds of Briony's return and at that moment they came. The front door burst open and her voice called, 'Hello?'

'Out on the terrace!' I called back.

She came swinging blithely through the sitting-room and stopped dead on the threshold of the french windows as she caught sight of Gordon.

'Mac!' she exclaimed under her breath.

I registered Lance's indrawn breath and Gordon's startled surprise. I said rapidly, 'Darling, this is an old friend of Daddy's, Mr MacIntyre. I forgot to tell you he was coming. He phoned one night when you were in bed.' I took a deep breath. 'Our daughter, Briony.'

Slowly Gordon held out his hand, his eyes still raking over the girl's face. Equally slowly she put her own into it. To my fevered imagination it almost seemed that I could see the twin halves of her struggling on her face for supremacy. She said, in a halting, staccato voice, 'How's Elspeth?'

'Fine. She—' Gordon broke off abruptly, staring at her in increasing perplexity.

Lance said through white lips, 'You can see how much I've been talking about you! The whole family feel as if they know you!'

I said raggedly, 'I suppose you've some revision to do as usual?'

'Yes.' She tore her bemused eyes away from Gordon. 'If you'll excuse me I think I'll go and get straight on with it.'

She turned and left us and Gordon shakily wiped his hand across his face. 'Ye gods, Lance, that gave me quite a turn. She has a great look of Ailsa, hasn't she?'

The last hope I'd been clinging to wilted and died. Ailsa. The final, unwanted proof.

'Has she?' Lance's voice was jerky. 'I can't say I've noticed.'

'Lord yes, it's almost uncanny. And yet—on reflection I suppose she doesn't really look like her.'

I said—because it would have seemed odd not to—'Who's Ailsa?' and noted Gordon's quick embarrassment.

'Oh—eh—just someone we both knew at art school.'

I had been right, then. I felt him take my arm. 'I say, are you all right, Mrs—Ann?'

188

'Yes thank you. I've been at a meeting all afternoon and it was—rather stuffy.' A blatant lie; there had been a fiendish draught blowing through the hall.

'Sit down anyway on this wee bench.' He guided me to it and there was a brief, uncomfortable silence. In desperation I broke it by asking, 'You're on business in London, I believe? Are you an artist too?'

'Of a kind.' He made an effort to be natural. 'Actually I'm a consultant designer. I'm down to arrange an exhibition of our work. We represent quite a few nationally known firms.'

'I see,' I said mechanically. 'It must be very interesting.' I glanced anxiously at Lance, who was staring unseeingly across the garden. 'If you'll excuse me I'll just go and see how the dinner preparations are progressing.'

Once inside the house I sped up to Briony's room. She was sitting at the dressing-table with her head buried in her arms. At the sound of my approach she lifted it and turned blankly to face me. 'I knew him,' she said dully.

'Darling, you can't really—you probably subconsciously remembered—'

'I tell you I knew him, and Elspeth too. Don't ask me how.'

'Well, don't worry about it.' I almost laughed hysterically at the inane advice. 'Write it down in the diary, as Dr Forrest asked you.' Mac, she had called him. The name sounded vaguely familiar. A scene clicked into place of

189

the three of us sitting at dinner at the Lanark Hotel and Briony's puzzled query, 'Didn't we come here once with Mac?' No doubt they had.

I said gently, 'Can you face joining us for dinner?'

'I'll have to, won't I? I can't just give in to it. Mother, am I going mad? Please tell me. I'd rather know.'

I caught hold of her protectively, pressing her head against my breast. 'No, darling, of course you're not. Dr Forrest told us there's a lot more of this illness about than people realise.'

'But this is the opposite of amnesia. Now I'm actually *remembering* things I shouldn't be able to. Sometimes they come into my head quite spontaneously and seem familiar, as though I've heard or said them before. It often happens when I'm looking at Daddy's picture.' Like thinking it was the best thing she had done? Perhaps that was when the initial seeds had been sown of my doubts about it being Lance's work.

'What other things have you remembered?' I told myself that it was important to be calm and clinical in order to report accurately to Max later.

'It's hard to say. Sentences flash through my head like a nagging kind of memory and when I reach for them they've gone. But I do seem to recall the words, "Promise not to say anything." And a bit later, "I can't take back a present, can I?"' She looked up at me frowningly. 'Isn't it ridiculous? None of it makes sense.'

'Dr Forrest may be able to interpret it for us. Write it in your diary now, before you forget, and we can tell him about it on Thursday. I'd better go and see how Mrs Rose is getting on with dinner. Come down when you're ready darling, and just be—normal.'

She gave a twisted little smile. 'Easier said than done, when I'm not.'

Mrs Rose of course had everything under control. There was nothing more to keep me from rejoining the men. They had moved into the sitting-room and I saw regretfully that their initial ease of manner had not been recaptured. Poor Gordon, this could hardly be as he'd imagined the long-awaited reunion. On my arrival talk became general and somehow or other we kept the conversational ball in play. Pat—pat—over to you—like a verbal tennis match.

Gordon said, 'I've never been in Suffolk before. Is it my imagination or are there really more twelfth-century houses to the square mile than there are anywhere else?'

'We're certainly very conscious of our history down here,' I agreed. 'The whole area was a thriving wool centre when the Flemish weavers came over. And did you know it was at Bury that the bishops swore on the High Altar to force King John to sign the Magna Carta?

191

The town's motto is "Shrine of a king, cradle of the law."'

'No wonder it seems old!'

'It's old, certainly. We have reasonably accurate records going back to about 500 A.D. and every new dig produces more evidence. We seem to have had the lot round here—Normans, Vikings, the Black Death—you name it!' I stopped, aware of letting myself run on, but Gordon and Lance seemed glad of my prattling. To my relief Mrs Rose tapped on the door to announce that the meal was ready. Briony, quiet and subdued, joined us and we went through to the dining-room.

Time and again during dinner I was aware of Gordon's puzzled glance going from Lance to Briony and back again. It was only too obvious that Lance himself was under considerable strain, evident in his clenched jaw and the tremor which shook his hand. But if he was bracing himself for Briony's next unconventional outburst, at least he was spared that. She spoke only when necessary and then in monosyllables.

For my part I hardly tasted the food. The meal seemed to drag on endlessly, but it was finished at last. Briony immediately escaped upstairs and as soon as politeness would allow I, too, made my excuses. Possibly without our inhibiting presence the two men would be able to relax. For myself it was a blessed relief to bath slowly and creep between the sheets.

192

Below me I could hear the low, intermittent murmur of their voices, and it was to that sound that, shortly, I fell asleep.

CHAPTER TWELVE

Lance had arranged to run Gordon to the station the next morning on his way to college.

'Don't forget I shan't be in for dinner tonight,' he reminded me as they were leaving. 'I have to attend that talk on cubism—they've landed me with being chairman. It won't be a late meeting, though. I should be home soon after nine. 'Bye, sweetheart.' He kissed Briony's unresponsive cheek and was gone.

As the sound of the car reached us, she produced from under the table the diary she was keeping for Max and handed it to me without a word. From the closed look on her face I deemed it better not to ask questions and opened it in silence.

The previous day, of course, had been her first entry, but an initial glance showed me that already something was very wrong. The first lines were what I had told her to write before dinner, about the sentences she 'remembered' in her head and her certainty of having met Gordon before. Then, halfway down the page, the handwriting altered completely and in this entirely alien scrawl I read, stumblingly,

193

another verse of the poem by Robert Burns:

> Till a' the seas gang dry, my Dear,
> And the rocks melt wi' the sun;
> And I will luve thee still, my Dear,
> While the sands o' life shall run.'

I lifted my eyes to hers.

'I didn't write it,' she said.

'No.'

'What does it mean?'

'I don't know, Briony.' I closed the little book and smoothed the shiny cover with my hand. It felt cool and faintly ribbed against my palm.

'Someone must have come to my room and written it,' she said defiantly, daring me to contradict the only safe solution.

'Yes,' I agreed numbly and added, clutching at straws, 'We'll show it to Dr Forrest tomorrow.'

She gave a little shudder, but after a moment she nodded and bent to kiss my cheek.

'Shall I give you a lift, since Daddy had to leave early?'

'No thanks, I'll catch the bus.'

'It's no trouble—'

'Really, Mother, I—want to be alone for a while.'

I had to let her go. There was nothing else I could do. So Gordon's visit had provoked another crisis, as I'd feared. Most significant of

194

all, it had confirmed the existence of Ailsa, though in my heart I think I'd always accepted it. After all, she must have been with us all these years just below the surface, continually reaching out for Lance's love. As long as Briony remained a child she was content to wait and simply be near him, but as she grew up Ailsa would become increasingly dominant. The strength of the headaches and resultant blackouts showed the force she was exerting to escape from the prison of Briony's other self. How long could the child withstand her? Was it possible, in this rational, scientific age, for a girl actually *to change into someone else*?

Twice I went to the phone to ring Max. Once I even lifted the receiver, but each time I turned away. Tomorrow. We'd see him tomorrow. I couldn't ring him every time I felt anxious.

Moira Cassidy tapped at the door. 'Mrs Tenby, do you happen to know if the invitation list is complete?'

I stared at her blankly.

'The list for the invitations to the Open Day,' she repeated patiently. Obviously her opinion of my intellect had not improved in the last week or so.

'Oh. I—haven't actually—thought about it.' I swallowed and tried hard to look interested.

'Mr Tenby usually keeps a dozen or so tickets back for his own disposal. Most of your friends are on the list from last year, but I just wondered if you might know of anyone who has been unintentionally omitted. I was hoping to have posted them all today. In fact, I did ask Mr Tenby last Friday to let me have the names, but he was dashing out to the chemist with Briony's prescription and must have forgotten. I thought he might have left them for me on the tape but I haven't come across them yet.'

'I'm afraid I can't help, Moira. I'll ask him tonight.'

'Very well, I'll hold them back for the moment.' She hesitated. 'Are you feeling all right?'

'Yes, thanks.' Did I really look so awful? As she went out I moved over to a mirror and studied my reflection critically. I did indeed look ill. My eyes were overbright, my features generally taut and strained, and a little nerve kept jumping irritatingly at the corner of my eye.

What had Max said, that day I first met him? 'The power of the mind can be devastating.' I could hear the echo of his voice above the endlessly lilting tune which was circling in my head like a ghostly refrain. And devastating it certainly was. It had destroyed Briony, it was destroying Lance and myself. Where would it end?

I thought with a sudden spurt of anger: There's no reason why we should all behave like puppets. We have minds of our own. We would have to fight like with like, a psychic battle to the death. But Ailsa was presumably

196

already dead and she was still stronger than we were. 'While the sands of life shall run': that would be beyond the point of physical death. Life continued and sought a new outer casing, that was all. Energy could not be destroyed. As Roger had said, it made biological sense. Perhaps Ailsa would continue to pursue us down the centuries.

Agitatedly I walked up and down the long room, my fists uselessly clenched at my side. Once I stopped at the painting and leant forward to examine more closely the small, perfectly portrayed figures of the lovers beneath the flowering cherry. Lance and Ailsa, hand in hand. There was no vestige of doubt left. All the years of our marriage that concept had been kept literally before his eyes, hanging on our own sitting-room wall. Was it any wonder the marriage had been doomed to failure?

I pressed my hands against my burning eyelids. Was this insanity? Did I really believe that the past could have such a stranglehold on the present? And what would Max say, presented with these new developments? Surely the multiple selves he had read about in his technical journals had all been divisions of one integral self, not undeniable possession by a totally different being. He had tried to rule out reincarnation on the grounds that there were times when Briony was undoubtedly herself and not the poor, miming shadow of a dead girl. Yet if two personalities could exist side by side in one body, was it not equally possible that two souls might have inhabited it from birth, perhaps only one of which was returning to earth for a second time?

I stopped pacing, trying to calculate when Ailsa must have died. Yet the only proof that she *had* died was in her presumed continuing existence in Briony. Lance had never told me what happened to the girl he loved, and even in the early days I had been too unsure of myself to risk asking. Nineteen fifty-eight seemed the most likely date. It was that which Briony had written on her sketch, and in Glasgow Lance had said, 'It's hardly changed at all in twenty years.'

Briony was not born until the autumn of nineteen sixty. 'I'm absolutely convinced I've lived before, and not all that long ago, either.' Obviously she had been ready to accept her parasitic intruder before I was. All I could pray was that she would never connect Lance with that previous existence, and that, I knew, was becoming increasingly likely. Her attitude when he had challenged Mark to the tennis match showed that.

The front door. I halted abruptly halfway down the room. Had Mrs Rose opened it to someone? I hadn't heard the bell. Before any further possibility could suggest itself, the sitting-room door opened suddenly and Briony stood there. Or was it Briony? I gazed at the familiar, unknown figure in horrified fascination, and over her shoulder caught a glazed glimpse of Jan's frightened face. She said quickly, 'I found her wandering in the High Street. I think she's lost her memory again. She doesn't seem to know who she is. Shall I phone for the doctor?'

I forced myself to say, 'Thank you, Jan, I can manage. I'm very grateful to you for bringing her home.'

'You're sure there's nothing I can do?'

'Nothing,' I said with finality. Nothing anyone could do. Jan disappeared. I didn't register her actually leaving, just realised later that she had gone. The girl across the room said, 'I don't understand. I thought Jamie would be here.'

'Not at the moment, I'm afraid. Would you like to sit down and I'll phone and let him know you're here.'

To my relief she apparently accepted this. I fled to the hall.

'Dr Forrest, please. It's extremely urgent.—No, I must speak to him myself. Mrs Tenby. Yes.—Max, it's happened again! Someone brought her home. I don't know what to do!'

'I'll come immediately.' The phone clicked in my ear. How soon was 'immediately'? It depended on the traffic. At this time of day, perhaps twenty minutes, with luck. Could I keep her calmly talking for twenty minutes?

As I went back into the sitting-room she said with a smile, 'I see he still has the picture.'

'Yes, indeed.'

'Was Mac here yesterday, by any chance?'

'Yes—I—yes. He spent the night with us.'

'I'm sorry to have missed him.' She frowned. 'I seem to remember catching sight of him, but perhaps I just imagined it.' The Scots accent was unmistakable. 'I'm sorry,' she added, 'I haven't introduced myself. I'm Ailsa Cameron, a friend of Jamie's.' Jamie again. Could she mean Lance?

'How do you do?' I said idiotically. She glanced at me in smiling interrogation and as I continued to stare at her blankly, prompted gently.

'You haven't told me your name?'

'Ann,' I said from a great distance. 'Ann Tenby.'

'Tenby? You're a relation of Jamie's?'

'A distant one,' I replied, totally without bitterness. 'Why do you call him Jamie?'

She smiled. 'Just an attempt to make him sound more Scots, I suppose. There's a poem by Burns—'Young Jamie, pride of a' the plain, sae gallant and sae gay a swain.' It was just a joke, really, and it stuck.' She moved restlessly. 'Will he be long?'

I moistened my lips. 'I'm not sure. I'm—expecting someone else, too. A friend of mine, Max Forrest.'

'Oh?' She was politely uninterested, caring

only about Jamie. A tap on the door made me jump. Mrs Rose came in.

'I was upstairs, madam, and I thought I saw Mrs Staveley driving away. Did—?' She broke off, her eyes widening as Briony turned towards her a face unmistakably not her own.

I said steadily, 'This young lady is waiting for Mr Tenby, Mrs Rose.'

Beneath her rosy cheeks the colour ebbed away, leaving red circles garishly standing out like the painted face of a clown. I added quietly, 'It's all right, I'll see to her.'

She nodded and slowly withdrew. A surreptitious glance at my watch showed barely seven minutes had passed since my phone call. On a flash of inspiration I said, 'Do you like music? We've rather a lovely recording of Ravel's *Bolero*.' As I spoke I was opening the record cabinet and searching feverishly through the sleeves. She made no further comment as I put the record on the turntable and switched on the machine. And all the time I was repeating to myself over and over, 'Briony! Oh, Briony!' with an agonised sense of bereavement. The girl who sat so composedly across the room had come from my own body, been at my own breast. Was there no lingering spark of remembrance inside her?

Sooner than I dared hope, Max's car skidded to a halt outside the window. I almost ran into the hall, but had no time to speak before Briony appeared in the doorway. I said flatly, 'Max, this is a friend of Lance's, Miss Ailsa Cameron. Max Forrest.' I carefully omitted the 'Dr'. There was a hint of impatience in her now, but to my relief Max immediately assumed control. He hesitated for a moment, glancing towards the stairs, before obviously abandoning the idea of attempting to get her to her room. Instead he took her arm and turned with her back into the sitting-room, seating her in the chair she had just left and drawing up a stool to sit in front of her. He was saying very gently, 'You're not feeling very well, are you, Miss Cameron? Rather dazed and bewildered? It would be as well if you had a little rest. You're really very sleepy now—very sleepy.' The girl's eyes had drooped, opened, drooped again. Her head fell back against the cushion. 'That's very much better. Can you still hear me?'

'Yes.'

'What is your name?'

'Ailsa Cameron.'

'How old are you?'

'I'm nineteen years old.'

'I'm going to start counting and as I do so you will become a little older. No, don't struggle. Everyone has to grow older.'

'No!' she whimpered, but his slow voice counted inexorably up to five.

'Now you are twenty years old. How old are you?'

'Twenty,' she repeated obediently. Then that

202

dreadful cry again: 'But I don't want to die!'

Tears were streaming down my face. Max said gently, 'Time is passing. Some years have now passed. What is your name?'

'Briony.' It was a strangely child-like voice.

'How old are you?'

'I'm seven and a half, and Daddy's taking me to the pantomime tomorrow!'

I put a hand to my mouth against the threatened rush of nausea.

'You are growing older, Briony. You're twelve—fourteen—sixteen. Now you're seventeen and eight months. How old are you?'

'Seventeen and eight months.' It was her normal voice.

'You're going to wake up now, but only for as long as it takes you to get into bed because you're still very, very tired. Now—one—stretch. You are beginning to wake up. Two—another stretch. Now you're awake. Three.'

Briony sat up slowly and rubbed her eyes, looking round her in bewilderment. 'I should be at school.'

I turned away to hide my streaming face. Max said matter-of-factly, 'You weren't feeling well so someone brought you home. Bed's the place for you, young lady. Your mother will help you upstairs and you will then sleep deeply for several hours.'

While he waited downstairs, I supported her poor drooping little body up the stairs to her room and helped her undress. She was too drowsy to ask questions. I picked up her diary from the top of the desk, and as I turned to the door I saw she was already asleep.

Max had come upstairs and was waiting on the landing. Without a word I handed him the diary and he read it swiftly. 'Events appear to be accelerating, do they not?'

I started to speak but suddenly my body was shaken by a series of vicious paroxysms which rattled my teeth and weakened me so drastically that I should have sunk to the floor if Max had not caught hold of me. 'I was expecting this. That is why I came upstairs.' Gently he steered me through to my own bedroom.

'I can't—stop—shaking!' I juddered. 'Please—help me!'

'It is reaction, that is all. You have been under a continuous and increasing strain and the body will only take so much before it rebels. Relax now. There. Close your eyes and breathe deeply as I tell you. In—out. In—out. That's better.'

The hypnotic quality of his voice soothed me and gradually the merciless buffeting ceased and I lay back exhausted. 'I'm so terrified she might hurt herself in some way.'

'She won't do that. After all, she's perfectly conscious on one level and well able to look after herself. The only danger is that she'll wander off again and we won't know where she is. It's beginning to look as though the only way to prevent that is hospitalisation.'

I struggled frantically into a sitting position, but he gently pushed me back. 'You're not fit to discuss it now. Also, it is time your husband started to face up to his responsibilities instead of leaving you to shoulder them alone.'

I said listlessly, 'Ailsa Cameron was a real person. She must have been the girl he was so much in love with.'

'That is undoubtedly a complication. The visit of this friend yesterday confirmed it?'

'Yes. Max, I can't send her away.'

He smiled reprovingly. 'You make it sound like selling her into slavery. It would only be for a limited time.'

'How limited? You said sometimes these cases last for years.'

'But you must see,' he insisted gently, 'that you will have no peace of mind if she is free to do as she pleases. Now that the initial break-through has occurred, such take-overs will become progressively easier and therefore more frequent.'

'I can look after her at home.'

'Perhaps, if she is sufficiently sedated and has regular therapy. But what of the strain on yourself—and your marriage?'

I said in a whisper, 'Either way, our marriage is probably over. Without Briony there'd be nothing to hold it together.'

He put one of his large hands over mine. 'Poor Ann,' he said gently. 'You continually underestimate yourself and between them, they're pulling you apart.'

'I suppose Lance will have to be told. I don't think it will come as much of a surprise.'

'He has been protected too long and at your expense.'

I said helplessly, 'I won't know what to say.'

'Would you like me to tell him?'

'Oh Max, would you?'

'Of course. As her psychiatrist it is my duty to do so.'

'He won't be able to come with us tomorrow, I'm afraid. He'll be at college.'

'In any event that would not be wise. It would interfere with Briony's treatment and I would not be able to give the matter the time it needs. Also, I feel that as things stand we should not wait even until tomorrow. He is bound to enquire about her as soon as he returns, and it would be asking too much of you to have to dissemble again.'

'He won't be back this evening until about nine o'clock.'

'That is excellent. If I may, I'll come about that time myself and we can have a full discussion. Now, I'm reluctant to leave you in this condition but I really must get back to the surgery. I dropped everything to come here, and I have some patients waiting.'

'Of course. I'm so sorry, I'd forgotten.'

Despite his protest I insisted on going downstairs with him.

206

'Till this evening, then,' he said, with his stiff little bow.

'Till this evening. And thank you again for coming so quickly.'

As the door closed behind him, Mrs Rose came out of the kitchen, her fingers pulling at her apron. I said abruptly, 'Please, Mrs Rose—please—don't ask me anything. Not now.'

'But I just—'

'I can't talk at the moment.' I turned blindly and pushed my way into the sitting-room. For a second I didn't register that the room was not empty. Then, just as the trembling weakness reclaimed me, I saw someone standing by the window. It was Edgar.

CHAPTER THIRTEEN

'Mrs Rose said you were upstairs with the doctor and asked me to wait in here. What's the matter, Ann? Are you ill?'

I said rapidly, 'Please don't ask me any questions. I don't want to think at all. Don't make me. Please don't make me.' I put my hands over my ears as though by doing so I could blot out my own thoughts, and as I started to sway I was again caught before I could reach the floor. Edgar's arms, surprisingly strong, carried me across to the sofa, where he sat cradling me like a child as I

207

lay jerking and shaking against him. I knew, of course, what would happen. I think I almost wanted it—it was a part of the analgesic my tormented body craved. In any event, when his mouth found mine I was ready for him, clinging tightly and returning in full measure the passion of his kisses. In a blurred way I accepted even then that he was only a Lance-substitute, but at least he seemed to want me, as my husband, in love with his dream of the past, had never done.

'Well!' he said shakily, when lack of breath had forced us apart. 'How do we follow that?' His finger stroked the line of my jaw with a gentleness that bordered on reverence. I did not reply. I was drugged with his kisses and blessedly held apart for a brief space from the necessity of facing what had to be faced.

He went on softly, 'You can't have any idea how long I've wanted to do that. I'd have made a move sooner but until lately you seemed reasonably happy.' He smiled into my blank face with infinite tenderness. 'I can hardly believe this is really happening.'

I said breathlessly, 'I'm using you, Edgar. You do realise that, don't you?'

'You can use me all you like, if using is the same as needing. Don't look so worried, darling; it's not as though we're hurting anyone. Neither Lance nor Cynthia care enough to be hurt.'

The truth of his words stabbed into me, but

208

my involuntary gasp of pain was lost as his face came down again to mine. I knew I wasn't being fair. I was perfectly well aware that I would never allow myself the luxury—and it would have been a luxury—of a full-scale affair with Edgar. All I needed was the soothing assurance of his love. A little later, already ashamed of my selfishness, I tried to explain but he put a finger on my lips.

'Let's not have any heart-searching, my love. I'm not asking for the moon.'

'But I must be completely honest,' I insisted miserably. 'The whole trouble is that I still love Lance.'

'I know that. If you didn't, you wouldn't be so vulnerable. For that matter, I suppose that deep down I still love Cynthia, too, but beating one's head against a brick wall begins to pall eventually. If I seem philosophical it's only because I've had longer to come to terms with it.'

I sat up slowly, belatedly aware of the fresh complications I had created. Suddenly, unreasonably, I wanted him to go. He seemed to sense my change of mood and accept it. Gently he put me aside and stood up.

'Well, I mustn't overstay my welcome.'

'Edgar—'

'Yes, darling?'

'Thank you.'

He smiled wryly. 'It was a pleasure, and I mean that most sincerely.'

'Bless you.' I put my hands on his shoulders and kissed him, gently this time. That tempestuous half-hour had given me a much needed breathing space and I was now able again to take up my life.

He had gone. I realised with a faint sense of shock that it was still only one o'clock. Almost prosaically I powdered my nose and replenished my lipstick. Then, presentable again, I went in search of lunch.

From time to time during the afternoon I went up to look at Briony, but she hardly stirred. With her hair all over the pillow and her lips gently parted she looked about twelve years old. Standing watching her sleep, the things I had discussed with Max seemed part of a macabre nightmare. Surely we couldn't really give credence to such fancies? And yet—

At seven o'clock Mrs Rose brought me some supper on a tray. I ate it in front of the television, grateful to have the time passed for me, opting out of original thought processes. And just before nine, rather earlier than I had expected, Lance came home.

He went straight to the cabinet and poured himself a whisky, holding up the bottle interrogatively. I shook my head. 'Gordon caught his train all right.' He gave a harsh laugh. 'I imagine it'll be at least another twenty years before he gets in touch with me again! He must have thought he'd landed in a mad-house.'

I laced my fingers tightly together. Oh Max, please come!

'How's she been today?'

'Briony?' I asked stupidly, stalling for time.

'Yes,' he confirmed with heavy patience, 'Briony.'

'Not too good, I'm afraid.' I swallowed past the knot in my throat. 'Actually, Jan brought her home at lunch time.'

He frowned. 'Jan did? How—?'

'She found her in the High Street, she said.'

'What the hell was she doing there?'

'I don't know. She—she was—amnesic's the word, I suppose.'

'One of them,' he said heavily, emptying his glass.

'How did the talk go?' I asked quickly.

'All right. There was a very involved discussion on the merits of Valmier and Férat—somewhat above my head, I'm afraid. It's not a form of art that appeals to me at the best of times. Ann—what are we going to do about her?'

I was saved from the necessity of replying, but not in the way I would have chosen. The door opened suddenly and Briony stood there. Except that it wasn't Briony. She said accusingly, 'You told me—' and then caught sight of Lance. Her face blazed with sudden radiance. 'Jamie! Oh Jamie, it's been such a long time!'

I had one glimpse of Lance's white face,

frozen with horror, before she hurled herself across the room and into his arms, covering his face with kisses. My mind was a pulsating void, blessedly powerless to inflict any further shockwaves. Then, with the suddenness of an explosion, Lance's immobility shattered.

'Get her away from me! Ann! For God's sake *get her away!*' He was fighting almost maniacally to free himself but she clung to his arm with the strength of desperation. Still in the grip of paralysis I could only sit and watch the horrific gyrations of their struggle. Salvation came to us in the shape of Max. Neither Lance nor I made any move to help him, but within minutes he had led the trembling, incoherent girl out of the room. I was still incapable of moving, but Lance spun round and strode out of the french windows. I assumed he'd go to the studio as he always did in times of crisis, but perhaps he realised his legs would not have supported him that far. At any rate he merely leaned against the stone balustrade, head down like a wounded bull, while he fought for the air his lungs seemed incapable of taking in.

Max reappeared, dishevelled and breathing heavily. 'Do you still imagine you can nurse her at home?'

At the sound of his voice Lance turned and came back into the room. Without a word he poured a glass brimful of brandy and handed it to the doctor. His face was as white as chalk, bruised with livid marks about the chin and mouth from the onslaught of Briony's kisses. Detachedly I wondered whether I was going to pass out. Max said sharply, 'Get your wife a brandy, too.'

Lance handed me a glass without meeting my eyes. I took a sip and felt the liquid rip like fire down my throat and into my churning stomach. He said to Max, 'How did you get here? Did Ann rub a magic lamp or something?'

'I was coming anyway. We arranged it this morning.' And in answer to Lance's raised eyebrows, he added, 'When I had to hypnotise Briony back to the present.'

Lance's teeth fastened convulsively in his lip. He said hoarsely, 'She was Ailsa, wasn't she?' His voice rose. 'Are we all going mad? I thought black magic was only a lot of eye-wash, but—'

'Black magic isn't involved, Tenby, nor any other kind. Just for the record, I presume Ailsa Cameron is the girl with whom you were at art school?'

Lance's eyes widened for a moment, then he nodded.

'You were in love with her?'

'I was.' He stared belligerently at the little doctor.

'What happened?'

'She died.' Bald and brutal, the words hung on the air.

Max said gently, 'And I believe I'm right in assuming that it was she who painted—that?'

My very heart-beats seemed to stop as I waited for his answer. He said expressionlessly, 'Yes. Damn you, you always suspected it, didn't you?'

I whispered through stiff lips, 'Oh, Lance!'

'Do you wish to say any more?'

'Only that it's none of your bloody business.' He poured himself another drink with shaking hands and drank it at once.

'I think it is.'

'I can't see why, but if you must know it was all based on a misunderstanding. When I learn the painting had won the prize, I tried to make her take it back, but she refused. She made me promise not to say anything. You can believe that or not as you choose, I'm past caring. And then she died.'

I moved quietly across the room and took hold of his arm. I felt that I owed it to him to transmit what little strength I had to help him endure this appalling assault. If he was aware of my coming, he gave no sign. He said raspingly, 'What has all this to do with Briony?'

'Merely this.' Max set his glass on the coffee table with infuriating deliberation and leant back in his chair, placing the tips of his long fingers together. 'You were immediately attracted to the child Briony. I learned as much from your wife. You had not come into contact

214

with children before, and it was a new experience for you, one that you had never expected to encounter. Because over the preceding—what? Four years?—you had subjected yourself to systematic brainwashing which had succeeded in convincing you that what you'd felt for this girl Ailsa was something unique which could never be equalled again.

'Undoubtedly,' he continued as Lance moved protestingly, 'you did love her, but not, I suggest, nearly as deeply as your memory now insists. For instance, until the results of the competition were announced you had made no attempt to contact her. Is that not so? Hardly the behaviour of an ardent lover. But after her death, you started to pile remorse, guilt, shame—all corrosive emotions—on to the memory of that love until it dominated your entire consciousness. It was at this delicate juncture that you met this child and her mother. I further suggest that it was the woman herself who attracted you, but you instantly repressed the truth, assuring yourself that you would remain faithful until death to your lost love. Instead, you deflected all this frustrated emotion on to the child and— because perhaps there was guilt even in detracting that much love from the past, you persuaded yourself that something in the child reminded you of Ailsa.'

Under my clutching fingers Lance still stood

unmoving. Max had paused, perhaps for corroboration, but none was forthcoming and he went on: 'Yours is a very forceful personality, Mr Tenby. Not only were you able to sway your own memories and emotions but you have considerable power of suggestion over others. The more you insisted to yourself that the child Briony was like Ailsa, the more in fact she became so, by a powerful combination of telepathy and thought projection. I am not suggesting that you deliberately set out to influence her, but she was malleable, unformed—and she returned your love. She was anxious to please you and thus, subconsciously in her turn, ready to be as you desired.' He paused again and this time addressed Lance directly. 'Can you accept this hypothesis?'

'*I* can't,' I said, surprising myself as much as the other two, who appeared to have forgotten my existence. 'Not that Lance changed Briony in any way. But I think you're right about the strength of his will, and if he subconsciously willed Ailsa back in those years after her death, I believe that she responded. I can hardly bear to admit it, but after this afternoon I have no doubts left. Briony and Ailsa are the same person.'

'Reincarnation?' Max asked softly, and I felt the shudder which went through Lance's body.

'Surely that's more plausible than the theory that he could simply by the power of his mind

216

recreate as convincing a replica as the girl I spoke to today.'

Very gently Lance detached his arm from my grip. He said jerkily, 'Your theories are fascinating, Dr Forrest, but I don't imagine you seriously expect me to believe them. As for my wife—' For a moment his eyes rested compassionately on me—'while I'm grateful for her support, I realise her own explanation is simply hysterical.' His voice changed, deepened and became urgent. 'Don't you see, both of you, that I can't accept *either* possibility and remain sane? The only important thing that none of us can deny, however we care to wrap up the facts, is that Briony has become schizophrenic. If any of the blame for that lies at my door, I deserve to suffer all the guilt complexes in the book.'

'But it is not schizophrenia,' Max interrupted quietly. 'Alternating consciousness is a different illness, known as hysterical dissociation or *grande hystérie*. I diagnosed that at her last visit but I was unable to discover the reason for it. I am now of the opinion that rather than one traumatic cause, the answer lies in the consistent force of will applied over the years. It was not a spontaneous dissociation but came about gradually.' He turned to me. 'You say you were convinced she was Ailsa this afternoon. To a certain extent you are right. The mind can convince itself of anything. In dissociation the basic, normally

217

dominant personality—which is Briony—is totally amnesic of the existence of the other. But the secondary self has all the waking self's memories and is aware of the two separate personalities. That was true of Briony just now; when I took her upstairs I questioned her on this specific point.'

'You talked to her about it? And she knew what you meant?' I stared at him in horrified disbelief.

'Exactly. I hope what I've just told you has convinced you both that she's urgently in need of specialised help.'

'You completely repudiate the possibility of reincarnation?' I challenged him.

'As such, yes.' He hesitated. 'However there is perhaps one other possibility we should consider briefly, in view of the particular aspects of this case, though it's not one I find easy to accept.'

'What is it?' I broke in.

His eyes met mine without expression. 'Possession,' he said.

I reached blindly for Lance's hand and his fingers gripped mine.

Max continued, 'As I said, my instinct is to reject it out of hand, but I must confess that it is occasionally necessary to leave a tacit question mark against that possibility. One case in particular that I read about in a medical paper appears to have no other explanation.'

'What was that?'

'It took place about a century ago, in the United States, and concerned two girls who lived in the same town. They never met and their families had no contact with each other. The elder one was subject to epileptic fits and was generally regarded as strange. She died in her teens, about a year after the birth of the second girl. This child, Lurancy, had a perfectly normal childhood but at the age of thirteen suddenly went into a cataleptic state. That is, she completely lost consciousness for a number of years, and to condense the story she eventually regained consciousness to all intents and purposes as the dead girl, Mary Roff. She knew everyone Mary had known and possessed her memories and her mannerisms.'

'And what happened?' I asked fearfully.

'She went to live with Mary's parents and they accepted her as their own daughter. In this case, of course, there was no possibility of telepathic influence since no contact had existed between the two families. Anyway, after about three months, she suddenly reverted to her previous self, went home again and lived a perfectly normal life thereafter, remembering nothing of her interlude as Mary.'

Noting our expressions of stunned disbelief, he added, 'You can read about it for yourself if you wish. I only mention this case because, unlike all the other instances of dual personality, this secondary consciousness seemed undeniably to be that of Mary Roff.'

'And what cured her was in effect giving in to it and actually living as that girl for a while?'

'I suppose you might say so, yes.'

'Personally,' Lance said brusquely, once more freeing himself from my hold, 'I don't know which theory I find the more outlandish. The only thing that seems clear to me is that until Briony has recovered, she very obviously mustn't see me again.'

'I suggested to your wife this afternoon that she should go into hospital. It would be impossible, now that her illness has developed this far, to keep her at home.'

'But we could have someone with her all the time,' I insisted desperately. 'Surely she needn't be sent away.'

Lance said heavily, 'If Ann wants her at home, then she must stay. We can arrange day and night nursing, anything you consider necessary.'

'And what will you do?' Max asked quietly.

'I shall leave the house. Temporarily, of course,' he added at my involuntary exclamation. 'As I said, we can't risk her catching sight of me again in this condition.'

'But you can't go!' I cried. 'Your studio's here, and Moira, and all your papers! How—'

'I could board at the college for a while. And if Briony remains in her room, I might even be able to continue using the studio.'

I put my hands over my face and began to

sob hopelessly. As Max had said, I was torn in half between Lance and Briony. It seemed I had no choice but to lose one of them. Obviously I couldn't allow Lance to be turned out of his own home, though I refused to admit the underlying fear that if he did go he might not return. But I must banish one of them, and to imagine Briony, alone and frightened in a mental hospital, was more than I could bear.

It was Max who came to me and led me gently to a chair. 'I know this has all been extremely distressing for you, Ann, but when she wakes in the morning Briony will be herself again. Unfortunately, we do not know for how long. Obviously she must not go to school or be allowed out of the sight of someone responsible, but she will be perfectly fit to attend her appointment with me in the afternoon. By then, you and Lance will have had an opportunity to decide what course you wish to take. Now if you'll excuse me I must go. I shall expect you at the surgery at four-thirty. Good-night.'

Neither of us answered him and presumably he let himself out. When eventually I moved my hands from my face, it was to find myself alone. Lance must have retreated to the studio.

Hanging on to the banisters I hauled myself upstairs. Briony still slept deeply. I knelt by the side of her bed and tried to pray for wisdom to make the right decision. I knew Lance would leave it to me. He was himself too deeply involved to be impartial and, as he had always stressed, Briony was my daughter.

It was some time later that, stiff and shivering with tiredness, I rose from my vigil and made my way to my own room. Lance had still not appeared, nor did he before I crawled into bed and tried to close my bruised and swollen eyes. Some time during that lonely, agonised vigil the decision must have been reached, because by the time I woke the next morning my mind was made up.

CHAPTER FOURTEEN

I phoned Max as soon as Lance had left for college.

'You have come to a decision?'

'I have, yes, but I haven't discussed it with Lance. Max—it really would be dangerous for Briony to remain in the same house as Lance?' I closed my eyes, waiting for his reply. If he confirmed the point, I had no choice but to go ahead as I had planned.

'In my opinion, yes,' he answered gravely. 'In fact, I consider separation is vital—for both of them. Those clothes your husband was wearing last night; they were too young in style for a man of his age. I found them very disquieting.'

I licked dry lips. 'I—don't think I

222

understand.'

'You ask me to accept that Briony is possessed by the—spirit—of this dead girl. I can only assume that Lance himself is equally possessed—by his own youth.'

'How horrible!' I whispered.

'But understandable. He feels he must be as she remembers him.'

'Then I have no choice.'

'To hospitalisation? Excellent. I can—'

'No. Max, please listen to what I have to say. I'm not asking your permission—I don't suppose you'd give it—nor even your advice, because it would be unfair to put any onus on you. I'm going to take Briony to Scotland—to Ailsa's parents.'

An exclamation burst from him. It sounded like 'Gott in Himmel!'

I went on quickly, 'They might refuse to take her, of course. I'll have to face that when I meet them, but it seems to me worth a try. I can accept the thought of her living with another family more easily than being shut away in a hospital with other disturbed patients. Most important of all, it might cure her as it did the girl you told us about, and more quickly than long drawn out analysis.'

'You realise she would be liable to revert completely in that atmosphere?'

'I'll have to risk that. In any event, it would be better for her than this nightmare half and half existence.'

223

There was a long silence and I braced myself to refute his arguments. But when he spoke it was only to say, 'Do you have any means of contacting these people?'

I relaxed slightly. 'The friend of Lance's who was here this week. I'll get in touch with him. I'm sure he'll help.'

'You realise of course that I can't condone this action?'

'Yes, it's completely my own responsibility. As I told you, Lance doesn't know. I'll leave a note for him, but if he phones you, as he probably will, please don't tell him where I've gone. He might try to stop me.'

'And what of Briony herself? How is she this morning?'

'She has another headache. I haven't quite worked out what to tell her yet.'

He said flatly, 'You're on dangerous ground, Ann. I'm not at all happy about the risks but I can see that from your point of view it's worth a try. Will you contact me when you learn the family's reaction?'

'Yes. Thank you. I was going to ask if I might. I don't know how long I'll be away. If they won't take her, of course, we'll come straight back and I'll have no option but to agree to a hospital. If they do, I'll stay nearby for a while in case she—reverts to herself.'

'Very well. Thank you for putting me in the picture. I shall be awaiting your phone call

224

with some anxiety. In the meantime—good luck.'

Carefully I replaced the receiver. The die was cast.

My note to Lance was deliberately vague. I wrote that I had thought of someone else who might be able to help Briony and was taking her to see what could be done. I would phone in a day or two and let him know when I'd be back. In the meantime there was no need to make enquiries about boarding at the college. I repeated the same story to Mrs Rose and detected the relief she tried to conceal. It was very obvious that she was now extremely nervous of Briony and I could hardly blame her. All that remained was to tell Briony herself.

I began casually, 'Darling, I suppose you realise now that you'll have to let this batch of exams go? You can take them later, when you're well again. In the meantime I think a few days away would do us both good. What do you think?'

'If you like.' She had a hand against her head.

'Daddy can't come with us, of course,' I continued artlessly. 'He has his work to finish.'

'Will he mind if we go without him?'

'He understands,' I replied hopefully.

'All right.'

'You just sit quietly and relax and I'll pack the cases.'

I was thankful she hadn't even been

225

interested enough to ask where we were going. In her present apathy she was also unlikely to notice that I was packing more of her luggage than my own. I felt sick with dread at the gamble I was taking. I knew nothing of the Camerons, not even if they were still alive, but faced with the equally unbearable alternatives to the plan, I still felt it was a risk I had to take. I could no longer sit back and watch Lance and Briony destroy each other.

After an early lunch we set off for Heathrow as Lance and I had done exactly one week ago. Already it seemed in a different lifetime, a 'previous existence', as Lance had once said. This time, unsure how long I'd be away, I left the car at one of the outlying car parks near the airport and we were driven to the terminal buildings in a mini bus.

At Glasgow we took a bus into town and then a taxi to the Lanark Hotel. The desk clerk remembered me and we were given a suite on the second floor. I had decided that Briony might not be well enough to use the public lounge and we needed more than one room in which to spend the days. Also, I hoped to arrange for Gordon MacIntyre to come and see me that evening when she was in bed, and I would not have dared to sit talking to him downstairs, where it would be impossible to listen for Briony. The suite was compact, a bedroom with single beds, a bathroom and quite a pleasant sitting-room, complete with writing desk and television set.

It was just after six by the time we had settled into our room and unpacked our night clothes. Briony was still pale and tired and agreed readily to my suggestion that she should rest for an hour before dinner. Thankfully I left her and returned to the sitting-room, where I had noticed a pile of local directories under the telephone table. There were several pages of MacIntyres but I recognised the address from our Christmas card list. Gordon answered the phone himself, sparing me what might have been a difficult explanation to his wife.

'This is Ann Tenby, Gordon—Lance's wife.'

'Hello there!' He was clearly puzzled by my call. 'Are you phoning from Suffolk?'

'No, I'm here. In Glasgow.'

'You are? I'd no idea you were coming up.'

'Lance isn't with me, just—Briony. Gordon, I desperately need your help.'

'Of course.' But there was a slight caution in the words. As Lance had remarked bitterly, Gordon must have wondered just what kind of a home he had been visiting. And now here was a hysterical woman he hardly knew requesting help.

I said quickly, 'You might have noticed Briony isn't well. She keeps losing her memory.'

'I'm sorry to hear that, but I don't quite see—'

'I know, and I can't possibly explain on the

227

phone. I'm at the Lanark. Could you possibly come along here and meet me later this evening—about nine-thirty?'

There was a brief, startled pause and I felt hysterical laughter welling in my throat. 'Gordon, I may sound mad but I promise I'm not. Nor am I trying to compromise you, believe me! I just desperately need to talk to you, as Lance's friend.'

'Of course I'll come. About nine-thirty, you said?'

'Yes, it must be after Briony's in bed. I booked a suite so we have a sitting-room where we can talk, if you'll just come straight up. Rooms 202 and 203.'

'I'll be there, Ann. Good-bye just now,'

So far, so good.

Briony agreed listlessly that she felt well enough to go down for dinner. Again the half-puzzled expression came and went on her face as memories assailed her which were not as recent as her visit the previous week. We ate, and the hands of the wall clock crept round. Seven-thirty. Eight. Coffee. Eight-fifteen. We returned to our rooms. Briony had a bath and went straight to bed. It was almost too easy. At exactly nine-thirty there was a soft knock on the door and I opened it to find Gordon, slightly apprehensive but as big and reassuring as ever.

'Would you like me to ring down and order you coffee or a drink?'

'Not for me, thanks. I've just finished coffee at home.' He sat down on one of the small upholstered chairs, dwarfing it. With racing pulses I plunged immediately into the story I'd been rehearsing in my head for the last twenty-four hours.

'Gordon, you said at home that Briony reminded you of Ailsa.'

He flushed and shifted uncomfortably. 'Me and my big mouth!'

'Will you tell me all you can about her?'

'Oh Lord, Ann, this isn't all my fault, is it? I mean, you haven't left Lance because—'

'I haven't left Lance at all. At least, only for a few days. Please, Gordon, it's imperative that you tell me. I'll explain why in a minute, but I promise it won't cause any trouble to Lance.'

'Well,' he began reluctantly, 'we were all at art school together, Ailsa, Lance, Elspeth and myself. We used to go round in a foursome and had some pretty wild times together, I can tell you.'

'What was she like?'

'To look at, you mean? Oh, a bonnie wee thing. She'd gorgeous red hair and a trim figure and she was bubbling over with fun. She was very talented, too. She and Lance often competed for first place.'

'Did she by any chance have a little mole beside her mouth?'

'Yes, she did. She used to call it her beauty spot.'

So Briony's 'self portrait' had been accurate enough. 'And did she ever call Lance "Jamie"?'

'Good lord—yes! I'd quite forgotten that.'

'Go on, then. What happened?'

'I'm not sure exactly, if you mean between her and Lance. One moment they were in each other's pockets as usual and the next she'd moved out of the flat.' So they'd been living together. The knowledge knifed into me but perhaps I should have expected it. 'Lance was very unforthcoming and I never asked him outright what had happened. Anyway, Elspeth and I became engaged about that time and we tended to spend more time alone together, especially as Lance no longer had a partner to make up a four. He won some big competition with that painting you have in your room, but he was very prickly even about that and refused to go out with us to celebrate. Then, I don't remember how, we heard somewhere that Ailsa had died. It completely knocked the stuffing out of us. She'd always been so very much alive. I remember being thankful that she and Lance had split up beforehand, so that it wouldn't be quite so hard on him, but he still took it very badly. Refused to speak of her at all, and after a bit we drifted apart. He'd changed, and I dare say I was too taken up with Elspeth to make the effort to win him back. Years later I heard of his marriage and wrote to congratulate him, and as you probably know we've kept in touch at Christmas ever since, though we hadn't met again until this week.'

'How did he seem to you?'

'On edge,' he answered quietly. 'As though something was eating away at his innards. I told myself he'd just grown older, as we all have. Then, when your daughter arrived, and seemed somehow to know me—I haven't been called Mac for years, but the crowd at art school always called me that—well, I have to admit I was somewhat less than comfortable.'

'I'm afraid what I have to tell you won't make you any more so.'

'Oh?'

Slowly and as matter-of-factly as I could, I recounted the facts of our original meeting, Lance's affinity with Briony and the terms of our marriage. I told of her increasingly frequent headaches, the strangeness Mark had mentioned and her eventual disappearance. And as I spoke I was resignedly aware of how insane the whole thing sounded. I finished flatly, 'So that's the position. I'm not convinced by all the medical rigmarole. In my opinion Briony is either possessed by Ailsa or she's a reincarnation of her.'

Gordon was staring at me, an almost comic look of incredulity on his face. 'You're seriously trying to tell me—'

'Very seriously. As you said, she recognised you and asked about your wife. You remarked then on how like Ailsa she was.' I unfolded the only concrete piece of evidence I had, the sketch Briony had labelled 'self portrait' which I had brought specially to back up my story. 'Does this look like Ailsa?'

He looked at it and shook his head slightly as though to clear it. 'It *is* Ailsa. She was always doing those lightning sketches. Where did you find it? Among Lance's papers?'

'Briony drew it.'

'*Briony?* But it says—'

'Self Portrait 1958. Yes, I know.'

'My God!' he said tonelessly.

'Will you help me, Gordon?'

'How can I possibly?'

I took a deep breath. 'I want you to go and see the Camerons.'

'*What?*'

As calmly as I could, I repeated the gist of the story Max had told us the previous evening.

'You want me to go to the Camerons and ask if they'll take her in?' he repeated, staring at me rather wildly.

'Yes. It seems to be the last hope. You do know them, don't you?'

'I've met them, yes. But Ann, do you realise what you're asking of these people? They lost their daughter tragically when she was only twenty. What was more, she was a brilliant artist and had a rosy future ahead of her. Can you imagine how they must have grieved at her death? Put yourself in their place. How would you feel if, twenty years later, someone you'd

232

never heard of suddenly appeared and said her daughter was a reincarnation of yours? I rather think you'd call the police.'

'Quite possibly, and that's precisely why I need you. I want you to go first and prepare the ground, explain what I've just told you. After all, they know you, they'd listen. Then, if they agree, I'll go and see them myself, and only after that, if we're all still prepared to go through with it, I'll take Briony along. You can take that sketch with you.'

'It seems so cruel,' he said in a low voice.

I leant forward urgently. 'Gordon, have you any idea what this is doing to *me?* I have to face the fact that I might possibly be losing my daughter too, by giving them mine permanently to replace theirs. I'm sure if they loved Ailsa as much as I love Briony they won't dare to refuse at least to see her. After all, I'm offering to give them back what they lost.'

'It's gruesome—unthinkable.'

'Yes, but it might be her only chance of recovery.'

'And if she does recover, what then? They simply have to let her go, having reopened all the old wounds? It would be like having her die twice.'

'I hadn't thought of that.' I looked at him bleakly. 'All right, if you think it's too much to ask I'll abide by your decision.'

'Surely there's some other way?'

'Only a psychiatric hospital.'

233

'Mac!' We had been so intent on each other that we hadn't heard the door open. Now, in her dressing-gown, Briony/Ailsa stood gazing delightedly at us. 'Oh, Mac! It *is* good to see you! How are things?'

In triumphant despair I turned to Gordon, watching the sweat break out on his hairline.

'How's Elspeth? It seems an age since we saw you. You were thinking of buying that wee Scottie pup. Did you get it?'

Gordon was staring at her in appalled fascination, his mouth twitching. 'Ailsa?' he said at last, his voice a croak.

'Oh come on, now! It's not been *that* long, surely?'

My bleak satisfaction at this living confirmation dissolved suddenly, giving way to panic. What could I do? Briony had slipped away again and Max was no longer within easy reach. I said sharply, 'Where's Briony?'

She turned from Gordon's discomfort and answered quietly, 'She's gone away for a while. She had a headache all day, trying to keep me in.'

My heart somersaulted. Not for one moment had I anticipated a coherent reply to my question. I remembered now that Max had told us the alternate self was aware of the circumstances. Perhaps after all there was a means of dealing with her.

Gordon broke violently into my confused thoughts. 'Is this some kind of game?'

'No game,' she answered calmly. 'Hasn't Mrs Tenby explained?'

'*Mrs Tenby?* You call your mother Mrs Tenby?'

She looked at him in mild surprise. 'Mrs Tenby is Briony's mother.'

I said with an effort, 'Does Briony know about you?'

'Oh no. She thinks she just has blackouts. That's what she fights against.'

'But can you come and go as you like?'

'It's getting easier all the time.'

'Ailsa—' I glanced at Gordon's rigid, horrified face. 'Would you like to see your own mother?'

'Oh, I would!' She clasped her hands together. 'I called at the house when I was up here last week but they weren't at home. I asked a milkman in the road and he said they were away on holiday. So I went to the flat but there was no one there either.'

'That was why you came to Scotland? To see your parents?'

'Yes, I wanted to let them know I'm all right.'

'If I try to take you to them, will you let Briony come back now?'

She hesitated. 'You mean that? You, Briony's mother, would let me go home?'

'For a while, yes, if your parents agree, but please go now and send Briony back.'

'All right.'

Painfully I held my breath and as Gordon and I watched unmoving, her face suddenly went blank. She stared fixedly ahead of her for a moment, then the little tremor rippled over her face and she blinked. She was Briony again. She glanced from me to Gordon, said uncertainly, 'Mr MacIntyre!' And then, fearfully, 'It happened again, didn't it?'

Gordon said in a strangled voice, 'I'll have that drink after all.'

'Would you ring down while I take Briony back to bed?'

As I led my daughter back to the bedroom, soothed her troubled questioning and wrapped the bedclothes securely about her, I tried to assimilate all the new factors which had arisen. There was at least a small crumb of comfort in finding that in her secondary state she responded rationally to questioning as Max had intimated. But so, I reminded myself, would the spirit of Ailsa if it were a case of possession. Our fantastic conversation had done nothing to confirm a diagnosis either way.

Back in the sitting-room, Gordon said, 'Did I imagine all that, or was it true?'

'It was true,' I said flatly. A waiter knocked on the door and brought in a tray with two glasses. When he had gone I added, 'Well, what do you say? Will you go and see them?'

'I suppose so, though God knows what I'll tell them.' He looked at me accusingly. 'You seem pretty calm about it, I must say.'

'Not calm, Gordon, just desperate.'

'Does Lance know about this?'

'Not where we are. I just said we were going away for a few days.'

'I presume you've taken her to a specialist of some kind?'

'Yes. He regards it as a case of dual personality, which apparently is a well-documented form of mental illness.' I didn't repeat my own doubts, nor mention the fact that most cases of alternating consciousness were splits of one self, not entirely separate entities. Only the strange case of Mary Roff and Lurancy was on a par with ours, and even there there were differences. All I could do was play on the similarities and hope the eventual outcome would be the same.

Gordon finished his drink and stood up. 'All right, Ann. I'll do what you ask, provided you promise to rescue me from my padded cell if they have me put away. And of course I can't vouch for their reactions.'

'You might be able to convince them, now you've seen her for yourself.'

'The trouble is I don't know what the hell it was I did see.'

'You can only try. If they refuse to see her, I'll just have to take her home and—let them put her in hospital.'

He stood looking down at me. 'You're a brave woman, Ann Tenby.'

'Or a foolish one. It's a calculated risk, but I have to try.'

'I think I can see that. Now, to business: if the milkman said last week the Camerons were away, they might not be home yet. I'll ring them tomorrow and let you know how I get on. Will you be all right in the meantime?'

I nodded, fighting the enervating exhaustion which always overwhelmed me after a tussle with my daughter's double.

'Then away to your bed and sleep easy.' He smiled crookedly. 'You're over one hurdle, anyway; you've managed somehow to enlist my services!'

'Thank you, Gordon.'

I closed the door behind him and leant wearily against it, trying to summon up sufficient energy to undress and get myself to bed. I wondered how Lance had reacted to my brief message, whether he had phoned Max as I'd anticipated. Somewhere in the chaos of my mind there were two minute causes for relief. One was the horrified violence of his reaction to 'Ailsa's' embraces and the other was the confirmation that he had not after all painted the picture which had always disturbed me so profoundly. The ethical consequences which were bound to follow this admission were for the moment beyond me.

I pushed myself away from the door, switched off the light and went through to the bathroom. In the mirror over the basin my face was white and strained. The face of a woman who has seen a ghost, I thought wryly; not only seen one, but talked to it.

In the bedroom I undressed by the light which came from the uncurtained window to avoid disturbing Briony. Across the street the bland face of another hotel rose in row upon row of windows, many of them lit and uncurtained. I could make out people moving about in the rooms and there was a curious, god-like sensation about seeing in one glance those in the rooms above and below that on my own level, to the left of it and the right. They were all enclosed in their individual little cells like bees in a honeycomb, but I in my detachment could see around them, above and beneath, things that were hidden from them. Idly I wondered about those anonymous people over there, about their hopes and dreams, their doubts, worries and perplexities. Had love proved as destructive for them as it had for us? For love after all was at the root of all our troubles: Lance's for Ailsa, hers for him, his for Briony, mine for both Briony and himself. All of us were helplessly turning the treadmills of our own imprisonment, powerless to save ourselves from the cages we had ourselves made.

With a sigh for the futility of it all I turned away and started to prepare for bed.

CHAPTER FIFTEEN

By the next morning I was overwhelmed by the enormity of what I'd done, and by what seemed the sheer lunacy of rushing Briony away from Max's expert care, to fling her into the midst of people who didn't know her and whom she didn't herself know. I almost phoned Gordon to tell him to forget the whole thing and that I was going back home.

However, my panic abated slightly when I realised that, rested after her long sleep, Briony seemed better than she had for some time, and even suggested that we should go out and look at the shops. Accordingly we spent the morning like any other visitors to the city, walking along Sauchiehall Street, drinking coffee and watching the crowds go by. We returned to the hotel for lunch in case Gordon should phone, but when no call materialised, I again fell in with Briony's wishes and we went to a cinema.

As we changed for dinner my ears were constantly straining for the first ring of the phone, and each time during the meal that the desk phone rang, I braced myself to hear my name called. The meal ended. We went back upstairs and watched television in our own sitting-room. Soon after nine-thirty Briony went to bed. By this time I was convinced that the Camerons had flatly refused to see either Gordon or me, and when the call actually came my hands were so fumbling that I almost dropped the receiver.

'Ann? Gordon here. Everything all right?'

'Yes thanks. We've had quite a reasonable day. How did you get on?'

'I feel somewhat as though I've been through the ordeal of fire but I'm more or less unscathed.'

'What happened?'

'I phoned the Camerons this morning and asked if I might call round to see them this evening. They were delighted, poor souls. They little knew what lay in store.'

'How did they react?'

'Pretty well as you'd expect. Flat disbelief— even anger.'

'I see.' My mouth was parched.

'However, I finally talked them round to agreeing to see you both. You needn't go alone first—I've explained everything as fully as I can. But I think I should warn you they've only agreed to see you out of sheer curiosity. They've invited us all for tea tomorrow afternoon—Elspeth and myself as well, to ease the tension. It's Saturday of course, so there'd be no problem. Will that be all right?'

'Fine. I'm glad you'll be there.'

'Elspeth suggests you come here for lunch and then we can all go along together. If that suits you, I'll come and collect you about noon.'

'Thanks very much. I'll tell Briony we're going to see some friends of Lance's and then we'll just have to see what happens. I imagine you told Elspeth the whole story?'

'Yes, indeed, as soon as I got back from you last night. I hoped it might clear things up a bit in my own mind, but I can't say it did. In fact, the more I think about it, the more fantastic it seems.' He hesitated. 'Have you been in touch with Lance yet?'

'No, there was no point until I knew if they'd see her.'

'Surely he must be very anxious to hear from you.'

'Yes. I'll phone him after we've seen the Camerons.'

'Right, I'll pick you up tomorrow, then, about twelve.'

The MacIntyres lived in a fairly large house out in the Bearsden direction. Elspeth was blonde and petite, seeming minute beside her large husband. The three children were also there, but from their natural manner I guessed they had been told nothing of the circumstances. Elspeth kept watching Briony with a slight frown, but the girl, completely innocent about the turmoil she had created, chatted and laughed unconcernedly and after a while we all relaxed. I began to wonder what would happen if Briony remained herself all afternoon. Obviously the Camerons couldn't be expected to offer unlimited hospitality to a complete stranger.

I need not have worried. Ailsa's home was in a small village called Drumlochhead and as we said good-bye to the three young MacIntyres Briony began to show her first signs of agitation.

'Couldn't I stay here with the others, while you go with Mr and Mrs MacIntyre?' she whispered. 'It won't be much fun meeting Daddy's friends.'

'You can't do that, you've been invited particularly. They want to meet you.'

She didn't argue any more. Perhaps subconsciously she knew it was no use, but I felt an uneasy sense of betrayal. In spasmodic silence Gordon drove between the large grey stone houses, through the narrower, less affluent streets and out into the countryside.

After some time Elspeth remarked, 'Here's the loch now.' The road ran alongside it. At this end was a small hotel. Some brightly coloured boats were bobbing about on the water and a group of people swam and sunbathed on the narrow beach. At the far end of the loch lay the village, sheltered to the north by steeply rising hills, whose lower slopes were splashed with the white of sheep.

'We're almost there!' The voice was Ailsa's.

I had been so intent on the scenery that I hadn't been watching my daughter's face. Now it was too late: she had gone. I saw Gordon's shoulders stiffen and Elspeth's head spun round, her eyes widening as she registered the undeniable change. Part of me was aware of relief that at least the visit would not be pointless. The other half wondered with superstitious fear if Briony would ever come back again.

'Are they expecting us?' she demanded excitedly.

I nodded in silence and she leant forward eagerly, looking out of the window. 'I mind the time I went sailing with Jimmie McGregor and the boat sank! Fortunately the water wasn't deep. Between us we dragged the boat ashore and Jimmie abandoned it in disgust. It was taken over by a family of moor-hens and left there for years. And yon's the tree I dared Jimmie to climb and he fell and broke his arm. I remember the spanking I got for that!'

I listened to her in a numb kind of misery. Only now was I realising that I was voluntarily preparing to hand my daughter over to someone else. Not that she *was* my daughter, but without her I had nothing.

Elspeth said suddenly, 'Can you tell me the name of my brother?'

The girl turned from the window. 'Hamish, of course. For shame, Elspeth! Are you trying to trick me?'

Elspeth did not reply and a moment later Gordon drew up outside a small neat cottage. Before I realised what she was doing, Briony had flung open the car door and run helter skelter up the path and straight into the cottage. The three of us sat in silence, waiting. Minutes passed. At last I said shakily, 'If we don't go and see what's happening I think I shall scream!'

The others moved at once and in a body, close together for protection, we went up the path. The front door was open and from inside we could hear a confusion of sounds—voices, exclamations and a soft sobbing. 'Have you any idea what you're doing to these people?' Gordon had asked me.

He leant forward and lifted the knocker and a moment later Mr Cameron appeared, ashen-faced, his eyes bright with unshed tears.

'Here's a fine welcome for you!' he exclaimed in self-reproach. 'Come away in.'

In the big kitchen which also served as living-room and, during the winter, bedroom too, Briony stood wrapped in the arms of a sobbing, clinging woman. There was no need for me to speak. Elspeth went forward and kissed Mrs Cameron's cheek in silence and Gordon introduced me. The woman lifted her ravaged face from my daughter's shoulder and murmured brokenly, 'How can I ever thank you?'

It had been as swift as that. They had had twenty-four hours to examine and exclaim over Gordon's preposterous story, and probably decided to reject it out of hand. But two minutes after the girl had entered the house all doubts were gone. What had been said between them I could not imagine, nor did I try. I wanted to tell them this was only a loan, that I must have Briony back as soon as possible. Of course I couldn't say it. And Ailsa—really I couldn't think of her as Briony in this setting—was so completely and immediately at home, helping her mother—the word came naturally to my mind—to lay the table, opening all the right cupboards and drawers for table linen and crockery, that I could only watch and marvel as the MacIntyres were doing.

Mercifully I remember little else about the visit. When it was time for us to leave, it became evident that Ailsa would not be coming with us.

'But—her things are at the hotel,' I stammered, unprepared for so abrupt a parting.

'Father will collect them in the morning,' Mrs Cameron said placidly.

We could only turn and go. At the gate Mr Cameron said gruffly, 'Mrs Tenby, I know fine there's a great deal to say, but you'll appreciate it can't be said just now. Our hearts are too full. Perhaps we can see you again before you go back to England.'

'Of course.' I added wretchedly, 'We haven't discussed her board yet.'

'Board?' He frowned.

246

I said haltingly, 'We can't expect you to look after her without—'

'Board for our own daughter? Not at all. I'll not hear of it.'

Somehow I stumbled into the car and we drove away. I was cold in the sunshine, cold and grief-stricken and desolate. Yet after all, I had achieved what I set out to do.

After a while Elspeth said jerkily, 'You must come to us, Ann. You can't stay in the hotel alone. We'll come with you now to collect your things and leave Briony's cases at the desk for Mr Cameron. If you pay the bill you needn't go back there at all.'

I tried to keep a veil between my eyes and Briony's belongings as Elspeth and I rapidly packed them away in the cases. A laddered pair of tights lay on the bed where she had dropped them before we set out that morning. I thought of how trustingly she had gone with me, never dreaming I was about to abandon her. What would Lance say, when I returned without her? Would I lose him as well?

The MacIntyre's daughter came out to meet us as the car turned into their drive. 'Where's Briony?' she asked in surprise.

'She's staying with the Camerons for a wee while,' Gordon answered tersely, getting my cases out of the boot.

'But I thought she didn't even know them!'

'She knows them now,' replied Elspeth. 'Away into the house, Alison, and take Mrs

247

Tenby up to the guest room. She'll be staying with us for a few days.'

Anticipating embarrassment and worse, Gordon must have spoken to the boys before we met again at the dinner table. They regarded me with puzzled curiosity but they asked no questions.

'There's a phone upstairs if you'd like to ring Lance,' Elspeth said gently. 'Give him our love and let him know you're welcome to stay here as long as you like.'

I closed their bedroom door, sat on the bed and dialled the familiar number. Almost at once the ringing tone was interrupted.

'Yes?'

'Lance—it's me.'

'Ann!' His voice was raw with anxiety. 'What's happening? Are you all right? Where are you?'

'I'm at Gordon and Elspeth's. Lance—I've just left Briony with the Camerons.'

There was dead silence. After a moment I said fearfully, 'Hello? Are you still there?'

'With—the *Camerons?*' he repeated, barely audibly.

'Yes. They—they want her.' My voice choked into silence.

'And you don't?'

'Please, Lance—you can't know what it's been like. But it worked for the girl in America and it might work again. If it—doesn't, we'll just have to do what Max says.'

248

'And you imagine they'll sit back and let you take her away again?'

'I don't know. I haven't dared to think that far ahead.'

After a moment he said expressionlessly, 'When are you coming home?'

'In a few days. I want to come straight away, but I must wait for a while in case Briony—comes back and wonders where she is. You do understand?'

'I don't understand anything. Not one bloody thing. I can't imagine why you didn't discuss it calmly with me instead of rushing off with her without a word.'

I said numbly, 'You said yourself it was better if you didn't see each other.'

'At least you could have phoned. This is the third day—'

'But there was nothing to tell you. I had to know first whether or not the Camerons would take her. We've just got back from there now.'

'Well, I can at least phone you, now that I know where you are. What's the number?'

I read it off the disc in front of me. 'You are all right, aren't you, Lance?'

'I wouldn't go so far as to say that. I've been nearly out of my mind with worry.'

'I'm sorry. I did tell you not to.'

He gave a harsh laugh which indicated just how foolish such a direction had been. 'Come home soon, Ann, for pity's sake.'

'Yes, darling, I promise. Take care.'

249

The days passed. Mr Cameron met Elspeth and myself and we settled things as best we could. I asked anxiously after Briony, but apparently she had shown no signs of reverting. It was arranged that Elspeth should phone them once a week to see how she was and I in turn would phone the MacIntyres. It seemed wise to avoid the tension of my direct contact with the Camerons. He also promised to phone Elspeth if Briony showed any signs of distress or returning to her own personality. For the rest, he asked after Lance, but only with formal politeness, and he continued to refuse to allow me to pay Briony's expenses.

Lance phoned me every night and I waited all day for the slender contact with him. At last there seemed nothing to keep me in Scotland. So I flew home alone.

Lance met me at the airport. He caught me against him and held me tightly, his face in my hair. Then, without a word, he picked up my case and led the way to the car. He had made the journey out by train and bus in order to retrieve my car from the car-park where I had left it.

As we drove out of the airport and turned along the motorway, Lance said abruptly, 'I wasn't at all sure you'd be coming back.'

'Why shouldn't I?'

'There isn't much to come home to, is there?'

For a stunned moment I thought he was telling me that everything was over between us.

Surely he couldn't be so cruel as to bring it up now, when the anguish of losing Briony was still so raw? But before I could brace myself for what seemed like yet another crisis, he had changed the subject and I had to collect my scattered thoughts to answer him.

'Did the Camerons mention me at all?'

'Only to ask how you were.'

'I don't suppose they'll ever forgive me, either.'

'Either?' I echoed in bewilderment.

'Any more than you will.'

I turned to stare at him but his eyes, hard and grey, were fixed on the road ahead. 'You're not to blame,' I said rockily.

'But I am. Your friend Max said so and he's right. It's been my fault all along. If I hadn't been so idiotic about the painting things might have been different, but after Ailsa died it was like an albatross round my neck. I felt it would be disloyal to get rid of it when she'd painted it for me in the first place.'

'You *wanted* to get rid of it?'

'Hell, yes. It was a tangible accusation, hanging there reminding me of what I'd done. Everywhere I went it followed me like Nemesis—you know that. "Lance Tenby, the artist of *Eternal Spring*".'

Yes, I knew. I too had shared in the haunting.

'I'm sorry, Ann. I just want you to know that.'

251

'Sorry for what?' I was unable to keep up with his verbal gymnastics.

'For everything, damm it. Everyone I've ever been close to seems to have been hurt in some way. I'm a regular Jonah. I suppose I refused to accept Ailsa's death out of pure selfishness. I wanted her back so that she could forgive me—tell me it was all right. And because I wouldn't accept it, I forced her to come back.'

I said whitely, 'Max said—'

'Max thinks with his text books, not his heart. I *know*, and I think you do, too. It would have been a hundred times better for you and Briony if you'd never met me. At least you'd still have her now. As it is, you have nothing.'

Obviously during my absence he had been tormenting himself by accepting the full blame for everything that had happened. Even more dangerously, he imagined he had also interpreted my feelings. I prayed for the wisdom to say the right thing, to bridge the chasm which had suddenly opened between us.

I said carefully, 'I still have you—haven't I?'

'For what it's worth.'

'It's worth a great deal, to me.'

'Don't be *kind* to me, Ann!' The violence in his voice startled me. He added more gently, 'I'm sorry. This is a terrible time for you and I'm only making it worse. Let's talk about something else. Edgar's been on the phone once or twice, fussing like a mother hen and wanting to know when you'd be back. I can't see what business it is of his, but I suppose he meant it kindly.'

'Yes,' I said raggedly. My control was in shreds. Any opportunity that might have existed to bring Lance and me closer in our common grief had disintegrated as soon as I touched it. Perhaps it would always be like that. I roused myself to ask, 'What have you told everyone, about Briony?'

'That she's had a breakdown and been ordered complete rest. Young Mark Staveley asked for her address so he could write to her, but I said it was better for her not to have any contacts with home at the moment.'

'What about Max? I phoned him from Scotland to let him know the Camerons were taking her, but that was about ten days ago. Has he been in touch with you since?'

'He certainly has. In fact, he's been making a bit of a nuisance of himself. He seems to have transferred his professional interest to me, now you've deprived him of Briony.'

'He was probably just keeping an eye on you for me. Perhaps if you really feel so full of blame he might be able to help.'

'I shouldn't think so. He can only be of use to people who *imagine* they're guilty of something. Ann—' another abrupt switch of topic—'would you mind very much if I disposed of that painting?'

'Mind? I'd be delighted!'

'You don't like it?' He turned in surprise.

'I hate it, Lance! I always have, but it seemed to mean so much to you and—and Briony.' I hesitated. 'I suppose it *is* legally yours, to dispose of?'

'Oh yes,' he said heavily. 'There's no doubt about that. Not only did Ailsa paint it for me originally, but she put a special clause in her will leaving me *all* her paintings—the word was underlined—'to do with as I please.' Imagine a girl of twenty thinking of making a will. Her lawyer told me she insisted on it before she had her operation. Almost as though she knew—'

'You shouldn't have any difficulty selling it, anyway.'

'No, that won't be the difficult part.'

'Then what—?'

'I shall have to admit first that I didn't paint it.'

I was aghast. 'But Lance, you can't! What will people think?'

'Exactly. It won't be pleasant but it has to be faced, firstly because otherwise the sale would be a misrepresentation and secondly because no matter whom I sell it to, I'd never be really free of it until that point was cleared up. That much at least I owe Ailsa. I should have done it years ago, but I was so stunned and mixed up and by the time I realised how famous it was becoming, it seemed to be too late.' He was silent for a moment, then he added flatly, 'But I also have my responsibility to you. You had no

254

part in the original deception and I've no right to expect you to share in the unpleasant publicity which is bound to follow.'

I started to speak but he lifted his hand fractionally from the wheel. 'Just a minute, let me finish. This business with Briony is a turning point. It has to be. Nothing will ever be quite the same again. At the moment you're too upset to think clearly or to see how things may turn out. I'm not rushing you for a decision, you must take your time. I just want you to know that if you decide you could manage better without me, fair enough. It's no more than I deserve. I won't make any public announcement about the painting until you've made up your mind. Then, if you do—go, at least you'll be clear of the disgrace. I'll make it quite plain that you were tricked along with everybody else.'

I said in a whisper, 'I don't need any time to decide. Do you really think I'd desert you, after sharing in all the glory for sixteen years?'

'No, I'd expect you to stay, out of loyalty. That's why I'm telling you there's no obligation.'

'I see.' It seemed to me that he had made up his own mind and was offering me a chivalrous loophole. Briony, whom he loved, had gone. In a way she was helping to repay Lance's debt to the Camerons, but to complete the payment the picture would have to go too. After that, and his admission of deceit, he would be purged, free after all these years. Obviously he wouldn't want me trailing behind him as a lingering reminder of it all.

'Do the Camerons know it's Ailsa's painting?' I asked, when I had a little control over my voice again.

'I don't know. In any case I'll offer it to them first, and perhaps a token sum for the royalties, if they'll accept it. That aspect of the business was always one of the most worrying.'

We were now approaching Rushyford and it was four o'clock. The streets were crowded with school children, dawdling along on their bikes, gossiping on corners, and no doubt comparing notes on the dreaded O- or A-level papers. I tried to turn the sob which escaped me into a cough, but Lance was not fooled by it. He said gruffly, 'I'm sorry. If there'd been any way to bypass the town I would have done.'

I didn't reply. I was realising how many inescapable reminders lay ahead—Fairfield Lodge, where every room was imprinted with memories of Briony; her friends who would keep enquiring about her, our life which, as Lance had remarked, would be so completely different without her. I wasn't sure you'd be coming back, he'd said. Had he meant that he hoped I wouldn't? It might have been the best way, a clear break, one traumatic severing from both Briony and Lance, rather than this painfully slow run-down to inevitable parting.

For the first time I entered the gates of the Lodge without the usual instinctive lifting of the heart.

CHAPTER SIXTEEN

Somehow the weeks passed. Every Sunday evening I telephoned the MacIntyres and each time they assured me that Briony seemed well and happy. Once, at the end of July, unable to keep away any longer, I flew up to Scotland for the weekend. Gordon drove me to Drumlochhead but I didn't contact the Camerons. I hung around waiting until Briony—Ailsa—came out of the cottage, laughing and talking to another girl. I didn't dare to approach her in case my unexpected appearance upset the delicate balance of her mind. Like an outcast I stood behind some trees, gazing hungrily at the unconscious girl, until eventually she went back inside.

The summer slipped by. Stella's picture was long since completed, the exhibition proved a great success and our own open house was held. For three days the house seemed no longer our own, with strange pictures and sculptures all round the walls and every room full of strangers consulting catalogues.

Edgar continued to drop in with less and less convincing excuses and I kept promising myself dully that I would bring the association to an end. But although our kisses were never again as passionate as on that afternoon before Briony left home, they were an undeniable source of comfort to my bruised and throbbing pride and I was loth to sacrifice them. Once or twice Lance appeared while he was still with me, and his greeting of Edgar seemed less affable than it used to be. Or perhaps it was only my own guilt that made me imagine it. For throughout this time Lance himself remained kind, considerate and very distant. He no longer wore the youthful clothes he had bought at the peak of the crisis, and he never seemed even to glance at *Eternal Spring* which still hung undisputed in its place of honour. He had promised not to hurry me, and he was keeping his word. The onus was on me, on how soon I could bring myself to agree to our separation.

And during all those long weeks our Sunday sessions were held with almost religious observance. It was on one of those occasions that I attempted to salve my conscience over Edgar's approaching dismissal. Cynthia had made one of her cutting remarks to Stella and me and instead of the usual embarrassed laughter, I said rather sharply, 'You know, Cynthia, I'm surprised Edgar stays with you, after the way you treat him.'

She looked at me in amazement, the pleased satisfaction at her latest witticism fading from her face.

'Or for that matter,' I continued bravely, 'why you stay with him, if you really despise him so much.'

She flushed slightly and the hard blue eyes, for the first time that I could remember, dropped away from mine. 'Are you losing your sense of humour, darling?' Her voice was not quite as confident as usual. 'It was only a joke.'

'Not to Edgar, I imagine,' remarked Stella, unexpectedly coming to my support. 'Ann's right. He must think an awful lot of you, to put up with you the way he does.'

'*Et tu, Brute?* Well, well! This is a day for surprises!' Her mocking glance invited us to smile, to change the subject, but we looked back at her unwaveringly and her colour deepened. 'The Society for the Prevention of Cruelty to Edgar!' she said with defiant flippancy. 'Can anyone join?'

'We'd be only too pleased if you did.'

'Oh for pity's sake, what's got into you two? Edgar knows perfectly well that I don't mean it.'

'Have you told him that?'

'No, of course not. There's no need.'

We didn't press the point, but I knew the warning had been taken to heart. Several times that day I saw her watching Edgar uneasily and on at least two occasions she bit back an obvious dig at his expense. It was now up to me to retire, to turn Edgar gently back in his wife's

259

direction. With luck she might be ready to receive him.

However, with my now customary lack of resolve, I delayed putting my decision into effect, and the delay proved fatal. One evening Lance returned from college earlier than expected and pushed open the sitting-room door to find me in Edgar's arms.

'I see!'

His voice was the first intimation we had of his presence. Edgar's arms abruptly fell away from me and I took an instinctive step backward. Neither of us spoke. Quite simply, there was nothing we could say.

'I seem to have been extraordinarily slow in the uptake.' His voice was hard and cold. 'How long has this been going on?'

Edgar answered steadily, 'It depends what you mean by "going on". I've been in love with Ann for some time, but—'

'And she with you?' Again the clipped, furious coldness.

'Lance, I'm sorry you found out this way. Personally I should much have preferred it all to be above board.'

'How noble of you. Then why wasn't it?'

'Ann's had enough on her plate without a showdown about this too. However, now that you do know I hope it can all be dealt with in a civilised fashion. After all, it's not as though you care for her yourself.'

An expression of white fury blazed across

Lance's face and for a moment I thought he was going to hit Edgar. Then, with a patent struggle for control, he said tightly, 'You seem to be very sure of my feelings.'

'It's rather obvious, isn't it? And you probably realise that Cynthia and I—'

'Will you please go?' We weren't prepared for the abrupt change in tone and Edgar looked startled.

'Now look, don't let's—'

'*Get out.*'

For a moment the two men stared at each other. Then Lance moved to one side of the doorway and Edgar, with a bewildered look at me, walked past him and out of the house. The sound of his car starting up reached us clearly in the stillness.

Lance said, 'May I ask why you apparently told Edgar to keep the association secret? Wouldn't it have been more honest to be open about it as he suggested, especially since I so obviously don't care for you?'

I said aridly, 'I'd no idea how he felt until a couple of months ago.'

'You certainly didn't appear to be in any doubt just now. Has Cynthia also been informed of her own emotions, or have you kept it from her as well? My God! To think I've always regarded Edgar as my friend!'

I roused myself to Edgar's defence. Obviously his defection mattered more than my own. 'He knew I was unhappy, and he just—'

'And how long have you been unhappy? For sixteen years? Were you afraid to tell me you'd made a mistake?'

'But I hadn't,' I stammered, hardly knowing now what I was saying. 'It wasn't a mistake, Lance. Please try to understand. And Briony—'

'Of course. I should have guessed. You would put up with a lot for her sake. Briony was happy and seemed to love me—' his voice cracked—'so you heroically bore your misery in silence. Now that she's gone, of course, it doesn't matter, which was presumably why you allowed yourselves to be rather less cautious than usual.'

'You make it sound so—vile.'

'And isn't it?' he flung at me. 'You, of all people, whom I'd always thought of as—'

'As what?' I whispered.

He stared at me and the pain in his eyes knifed into me. As I watched, the anger dropped suddenly away from him and he seemed to sag. 'It doesn't matter. You were right. Nothing matters any more.' He turned on his heel and a moment later I heard the front door and his car. Like a blind person I put my hands out in front of me and felt my way across the room. My desolation, my isolation, was complete. Even Edgar had been taken away from me before I was ready to stand alone. And now Lance—but I didn't dare to think about Lance.

The hours crawled by and he didn't come back. Mrs Rose knocked to enquire if he would be in for dinner. We waited till eight o'clock and then I ate alone. That is, I mechanically put food into my mouth and forced myself to swallow a little. Still the painting hung on the wall as though gloating that now the havoc it had wrought was complete. Briony had gone. Lance had gone. And, irony of ironies, it was I, who had always hated it, who was the only one left with it.

I had to get away from its luminous magnetism and, like Lance had so often done, I took refuge in the studio. For a while I sat on the chair with my arms across the table and my head buried in them, as I'd found Lance that night when Briony had first disappeared. Remembering that night, I started to tremble. Outside, the air grew denser and deeper blue. Midges hovered in a soft blue cloud, the scent of the stocks in the shrubbery flooded the small room with almost unbearable sweetness.

I switched on the light, watching the garden beyond the window leap backwards into contrasting darkness. Dully I looked around this room where I had never been without Lance. It probably knew him better than I did.

I rose stiffly to my feet and moved over to the heap of canvases stacked against the wall, flicking unseeingly through them and remembering the times he had painted them.

263

To my mind they were much more arresting, more humane, than the one which had erroneously established his name. I turned from them to the pile of rough sketches on the table. It was here that I'd seen the sketch of Ailsa that day. With the dull pain which was now permanent I wondered if he had kept it. I started to turn over the sheets and stopped suddenly. A tide of burning heat washed slowly over me and ebbed away, leaving me shivering. I was looking not at the elfin face of Ailsa but at my own, yet with an expression on it that I hadn't realised anyone had ever seen. The essential features were the same as those which confronted me in the mirror every day—short, softly curling hair, wide eyes, vulnerable mouth. But the whole aura conjured up by those few skilful strokes was one of tenderness. The eyes were soft and full of love, the mouth gently curved. Was that how I looked when he made love to me? But our infrequent lovemaking had always been in the dark. Was it then as he imagined I would look, if I loved him? As, perhaps, he hoped I might one day look?

With the sketch in my hands I sank slowly on to the chair. 'I suggest' Max had said, in his dry, professional voice, 'that it was the woman herself who attracted you, but you repressed the truth.' *Could* it have been the truth? And if so, when had he realised it himself? That night here when we had loved each other so spontaneously? Or when I went away with Briony and he thought I might not return? Then why hadn't he told me, instead of pushing me even further away from him? Why in heaven's name hadn't he said anything?

Tenderly I put the sketch on the table and after a moment, laid my cheek down on it and closed my eyes.

'Ann! Oh, thank God! When you weren't in the house I was sure you must have gone!'

I turned my face away from the light and saw the paper on which I'd been resting. I sat up, staring down at it. Lance hadn't noticed it and slowly, inconspicuously, I turned it face down. He sat down opposite me on the stool where Stella had once sat.

'Ann, I'm sorry. I'd no right to speak to you like that. I don't know why I made such a fuss, when I'd already given you permission to go if and when you were ready. I suppose it just hadn't occurred to me that you wouldn't go alone. Edgar's a decent enough fellow really, and he's had a raw deal with Cynthia. One day—' he smiled crookedly—'I might even manage to be glad for him.'

'But you can't now?'

Slowly I turned over the sketch on the table and heard his indrawn breath.

'When did you draw this?'

'A few weeks ago. Why? Doesn't it fit in with Edgar's ideas?' He stared down at his hands, gripped tightly together between his knees. 'I

265

hadn't intended to go into all this—there didn't seem to be much point—but now you've seen that I might as well tell you. I suppose you have a right to know.'

'Yes?' I had expected the moment of truth before. This time I wouldn't anticipate it, in case the mere fact of doing so dispersed it.

He said in a low voice, 'I still can't say I'm all that fond of Max, but I have to admit he knows what he's talking about. All that jargon about building up my love for Ailsa with guilt, and so on—it was pretty near the mark. And he was right about my not allowing myself to be interested in you in that way. It was safer to opt for Briony. And having convinced myself of my own undying love for someone else, I had to assume the same for you. It was a kind of double indemnity. Of course, I wasn't aware of all these ramifications at the time.' He gave a mirthless little laugh. 'It's just my luck that I should only find out you weren't still firmly committed to the past by discovering that you'd fallen for Edgar.'

I said steadily, 'Lance, I'm not, and I have never been in love with Edgar. He knows that.'

'But he said—'

'That he loved me, and that was what I needed. Quite desperately.' He made some movement but I went on quietly, 'You still haven't got it quite right. I was never committed to the past. My love for Michael died even before he did. It was schoolgirl

266

infatuation, really, nothing more. Our marriage was a disaster. I've never told anyone this before and I wouldn't tell you now except that it seems we've both been going around blindfold for too long. It was rather ironic, really, that while the love of your life was for Ailsa, mine was for you.'

'You mean—all this time—?'

'Yes, all this time.'

'But—' He seemed to have difficulty speaking. 'You agreed—originally—'

'To the marriage of convenience? I'd no choice, had I? It was all you offered me: take it or leave it.'

He reached blindly for my hand and gripped it. I could actually feel the bones crushing together as though they would splinter. He said in a choked voice, 'All these years, and I never—'

I said softly, 'With luck there are still plenty of years left.'

I don't think either of us had any idea what time it was when, through the mists of sleep, we heard Mrs Rose calling.

'Mr Tenby, sir! Are you there? Madam?'

'Oh lord!' Lance propped himself up and looked down at me. 'All is discovered, my darling! We are undone!'

'Are you there, Mr Tenby?' Her voice was nearer.

'Yes, Rosie, we're here.' He pulled on his slacks and opened the door. Beyond him from where I lay, I could see the silver sheen of dew heavy on the grass. Then her voice came again, close at hand.

'It's the phone for you, sir. Mr MacIntyre. Says it's urgent.'

I sat up suddenly, fumbling for my clothes, hearing Lance's voice change. 'What time is it, for pity's sake?'

'Just gone five, sir. I couldn't think where you were—'

He brushed past her and ran barefoot over the wet grass, I close behind him.

'Gordon? What—? Oh *no!* No!'

'What is it?' I gasped, pulling the receiver away from his ear so I could hear the voice at the other end of the wire.

'—the Western,' Gordon was saying. 'They're operating right away. Old Cameron signed the consent form.'

I snatched the phone. 'Gordon, what's happened?'

'Appendicitis, Ann. It's—all right. She's in good hands. I'll have a car at the airport waiting for you.'

I turned to Lance, shivering and sick. He said flatly, 'That's how Ailsa died.'

'Not twice,' I said judderingly. 'Please God, not twice.'

I moved through the following hours with the fluidity of a dream. Lance loved me. Briony was even now undergoing an operation. Neither fact, though I repeated them endlessly to myself, seemed believable. Occasionally, in the senseless repetition, they wound themselves about each other unintelligibly. Lance was having an operation. Briony loved me. But was it Briony, lying there in a hospital bed, or Ailsa, as it had been the last time? And if it was still Ailsa, was the eventual outcome predestined? I knew, though he made no comment, that this was Lance's great fear.

Heathrow seemed almost familiar now, but still blessedly impersonal, still carrying on its normal daily business despite the dizzy swing from heights to depths which plagued our lesser lives. The plane rose gracefully into the cloudless blue of a perfect summer day. Would it be Briony's last?

CHAPTER SEVENTEEN

There was a burning sensation behind my eyes. Beside me, Lance's hands gripped the wheel of the hired car in a desperate attempt to conceal from me the shaking which had claimed him. Appendicitis wasn't usually serious, I assured myself. Even so, there had been no mistaking the concern in Gordon's voice and Lance's reaction had been devastating. Was it because all this had happened before?

A lorry swooshed past with a warning blare of its horn. I said automatically, 'Careful,

269

darling. Keep to the left.'

The hospital loomed up, grey and forbidding, and the stomach-churning smell of disinfectant and cooking reached out for us. In the foyer Mr and Mrs Cameron came forward to greet us, dumbly reaching for our hands.

I heard myself say, 'Where is she?'

It was Lance who answered me. 'First floor. Robert Burns Ward.'

My startled eyes went to the Camerons for confirmation and, equally startled, they nodded. Lance caught my hand and together we ran up the shallow flight of stairs.

'Mr and Mrs Tenby? It's all right for you to go in now. She's at the far end, in the bed behind the screen.'

We hurried between the rows of high iron beds, each with its chart at the foot, our eyes fixed on the screen in the far corner. Let her be all right! Oh, let her be all right!

She looked pathetically small and defenceless lying there. Her eyes were closed, the lashes casting shadows on her round cheeks. And as we stood looking down at her, a voice—was it just in my head?—said softly, 'Jamie! I knew fine you'd come!'

Lance pulled a chair up to the bed and took hold of her hand.

'Listen carefully, darling. You know that I loved you; nothing can change that. I owe you a great deal, and I intend to put the record straight about the painting, but I'm sorry if my

270

selfishness was responsible for bringing you back. You're free now, Ailsa, and so am I. We've gone full circle. But Briony mustn't be hurt any more because of us. Ann and I love her very much and we want her back. Permanently. You do understand, don't you?'

I moved over to him, putting my hand on his shoulder, and we both stared intently down at the face on the pillow. And as we watched, the little tremor came and went for the last time. Briony stirred, moved her head slightly, and her eyes flickered open.

She murmured drowsily, 'Oh, there you are. I dreamt—' And then her eyes opened fully and she looked about her in growing fear. 'Daddy, where am I? What's happening?'

I said brokenly, because Lance couldn't speak, 'It's all right, darling. Everything's going to be all right now.'

Down in the foyer the Camerons were waiting. Lance said exuberantly, 'It's all right! She's going to be all right!'

'Aye, we know that,' Mr Cameron replied gravely. 'It was a straightforward case, thank God. Not like Ailsa's.'

Not like Ailsa's. Did that mean—could they already know—?

Mrs Cameron said quietly, 'I'm glad you've got your lassie back, Mrs Tenby. We lost ours a long time ago. We must keep remembering that.'

Lance said with difficulty, 'Mrs Cameron,

271

there's something I must tell you. I hardly know how, after all this time.'

'If it's about the painting, spare yourself, Lance. We've known all along.'

'You—?'

'Aye. But it was the way Ailsa wanted it, and no concern of ours.'

The old man's eyes softened. 'If you've been blaming yourself unduly you can stop now. It may have put you on the first rung of the ladder, but you've climbed to the top on your own merit.'

'Will you at least let me give it to you? I've had no right—'

'We don't want it, laddie. It's not a happy painting. It frightened us when she was working on it. It almost seemed as though she expected to die.' Hadn't Max said something like that? 'I doubt it's brought you and your family much happiness. Do what you like with it. We want no part of it. However, if you've some of her other canvases you could spare—'

'Of course. I'll go through them as soon as we get home.'

'What will you do with it?' I asked Lance later. We were in the bedroom I had used before at the MacIntyres'.

'Hand it over to Christie's, I think, and let them get the best price they can for it. Then I'll send the cheque to charity. But first I'll have to admit I didn't paint it.' He went over to the window and stood staring out at the distant

272

hills. 'Dear old Scotland. It's right this business should be finished with here, where it all started.'

Elspeth's voice reached us from the foot of the stairs. 'Dinner's ready!'

'And so am I!' Lance commented. 'I don't know when I last felt so hungry. It's probably relief from all the strain and stress. I'm actually free of it, after twenty years!'

He came across and kissed me gently. 'Thanks for waiting for me, darling.'

My heart was too full to reply. Hand in hand we went downstairs to dinner.

We hope you have enjoyed this Large Print book. Other Chivers Press or G.K. Hall & Co. Large Print books are available at your library or directly from the publishers.

For more information about current and forthcoming titles, please call or write, without obligation, to:

Chivers Press Limited
Windsor Bridge Road
Bath BA2 3AX
England
Tel. (01225) 335336

OR

G.K. Hall & Co.
P.O. Box 159
Thorndike, Maine 04986
USA
Tel. (800) 223–2336

All our Large Print titles are designed for easy reading, and all our books are made to last.